PARADISE

CITY

THE BIG EMPTY

PARADISE

CITY

BY
J.B. STEPHENS

razOr
bill
NEW YORK

The Big Empty 2: Paradise City

RAZORBILL

Published by the Penguin Group
Penguin Young Readers Group
345 Hudson Street, New York, New York 10014, U.S.A.
Penguin Group (USA) Inc., 375 Hudson Street, New York, New York 10014, U.S.A.
Penguin Books Canada Ltd, 10 Alcorn Avenue, Toronto, Ontario, Canada M4V 3B2
(a division of Pearson Penguin Canada, Inc.)
Penguin Books Ltd, 80 Strand, London WC2R 0RL, England
Penguin Ireland, 25 St Stephen's Green, Dublin 2, Ireland
(a division of Penguin Books Ltd)
Penguin Group (Australia), 250 Camberwell Road, Camberwell, Victoria 3124,
Australia (a division of Pearson Australia Group Pty Ltd)
Penguin Books India Pvt Ltd, 11 Community Centre, Panchsheel Park,
New Delhi – 110 017, India
Penguin Group (NZ), Cnr Airborne and Rosedale Roads, Albany, Auckland,
New Zealand (a division of Pearson New Zealand Ltd)
Penguin Books (South Africa) (Pty) Ltd, 24 Sturdee Avenue, Rosebank,
Johannesburg 2196, South Africa

Penguin Books Ltd, Registered Offices: 80 Strand, London WC2R 0RL, England

10 9 8 7 6 5 4 3 2 1

Interior design by Christopher Grassi

Library of Congress Cataloging-in-Publication Data is available

Printed in the United States of America

ONE

SOMEWHERE OUTSIDE THE FENCE HE WAS PATROLLING, THE OLD world that Michael knew was gone.

Both worlds, actually. The happy, civilized place of constant electricity and food and *people* before Strain 7, and the life afterward he had managed to carve out for himself—working for his dad, growing his career in the post-virus world. *Thanks to Maggie.* Outside the fence, survivalists and the Slash roamed the wilds of the Big Empty, the depopulated waste between the two coasts that was once the breadbasket of America. Outside the fence, soldiers of the MacCauley administration patrolled to make sure everyone had evacuated the Midwest, and life in the cities on the coasts was sad and hopeless.

But in here, within the confines of Novo Mundum, was

literally a whole new world: an ideal community of scientists and doctors and dreamers and healers, trying to do *more* than survive, trying to keep alive mankind's nobler pursuits.

It was Indian summer, a golden early week of November. Many of the trees were already bare, letting the gentle, warming sun reach the three of them like a friendly pat on the back. Leaves crunched underfoot and filled the air with brown, moist, earthy smells. Paradise, in a very American kind of way.

Michael couldn't remember being this happy in a long time. Back in New York, even though he'd had a good job working for his father's security systems company, life still had been frightening and tough. Food coupons. Meat rations. And MacCauley soldiers everywhere, trained to shoot on sight anyone who broke the new laws, no matter how minor the law, no matter how desperate the perpetrator. Like Maggie, who was set up by her *friends* while they stole from a store.

When they fled to the "freedom" of the Big Empty, all Michael and Maggie had found were empty cities, dry acres of dirt gone to weed and dust in a land that had lost all of its happy endings.

But not here.

Here there was hope—fifteen hundred people working together to keep art, poetry, music, and science alive, free from an oppressive government; an oasis in the equally oppressive Big Empty. Here there were microscopes and concerts and computers and gardens and laughter and a *community spirit* that seemed to have abandoned the rest of the United States.

And here also was Liza. The daughter of Dr. Paul Slattery, who led Novo Mundum with his brother, Frank.

He was just picturing her laugh, lips wide open and large brown eyes on his—when Gabe snapped a twig with his boot.

"Hey, Bishop, snap out of it." But the ex-soldier was smiling. "We're here to patrol, not daydream."

Finch, on the other side of him, jabbed Michael in the ribs with the butt of his rifle. "Yeah—attention, soldier!"

Michael grinned.

"Didn't you just *break up* with your last girlfriend, like, three weeks ago?" Of the two U.S. Army ex-soldiers, Gabe was definitely the more outgoing. Michael got along great with both of them, but Finch was a little quiet, a little more brooding than the friend he'd defected with.

"Tried to break up with her, had my life ruined by her, traveled a thousand miles with her, really broke up with her, got ditched by her," Michael said, sighing. It was still a little recent to be too lighthearted about, but Liza was definitely helping the Maggie memories fade. Liza had all the good qualities of his ex-girlfriend: sexy, warm, attentive—without all of the annoying parts. Like Maggie's complete disconnection from reality, for instance.

"He's sleeping his way to the top," Finch said. "Straight to Dr. Slattery's third-hand man."

Michael actually found himself blushing and focused on checking his own gun so the other two wouldn't see.

He had never even *held* a gun before Novo Mundum, and now here he was, assigned his own double-barreled shotgun, patrolling the borders of his new home. Vital. Important.

Gabe's radio crackled. He picked it up and played with the buttons, frowning. "That's strange; base never uses that channel—" Short, curt masculine phrases buzzed meaninglessly through the speaker, becoming clear for a second as Gabe adjusted the dial. Someone giving orders.

Michael's eyes widened as his two friends' faces hardened, all three coming to the same conclusion: soldiers.

MacCauley-style soldiers.

He felt his heart drain out through his stomach. *No. Not now.* He had found something he hadn't even realized he was missing here, among friends—and now the Big Guns were coming in to destroy it. It was like he had to keep on running. . . .

Finch immediately touched his own headset. "Finch to base. We've picked up signals from another radio— think it's an enemy patrol. Over."

"Copy that," came the clear response—though the person sounded anxious. "A trip wire was just set off . . . southeast of the clock tower, about a quarter klick. They bypassed the road—*how did they know the way?*" There was panic in the voice of the person at the other end before he recovered himself. "Can't get any visuals yet; the cover is too dense. All available patrols are to check it out. Over."

Michael listened intently, trying not to feel useless. He wanted to *do* something. Anything.

"Copy. Gabe, Michael, and I are the closest. We're going now. Over."

"Maintain radio silence until a-okay or reinforcements needed. Over and out."

"Any idea how many there are, Gabe?" Finch asked, turning to the other two.

"Sounded like a basic scout. Four, maybe five."

"I guess we should go take them out," Michael said, trying not to sound nervous. Actually, he realized he wasn't *nervous*. He was shaking with rage, a desire to go out and *get rid of* the soldiers out there, to prevent exactly what everyone at Novo Mundum had feared from the beginning.

An invasion.

TWO

JONAH TIGHTENED A BIG COPPER PIPE AS DELICATELY AS HE COULD with the wrench wrapped in duct tape. This might be one of the most advanced research facilities in America—maybe *the* most, if none of the others were left—but there was somehow no one in the department, or in all of Novo Mundum, who knew anything about plumbing. Or had the right tools for it. And while they had chosen Jonah to join them for his brilliance and vision, they were over-joyed when he revealed that he could also do a lot of basic handyman work.

He'd had to, growing up. Jonah's mom and dad rarely stopped fighting long enough to get anything done around the house. And his dad was constantly breaking things. Things Jonah could fix, like the stuck pipes after his dad kicked them. Things he *couldn't* fix—like the time his dad threw the microwave out their window.

But now he was safe from his parents, from Atlanta, from the whole world of Strain 7. Novo Mundum had taken him in and protected him from all that and he would do anything for them, even fix the pipes. He whistled a little as he worked.

Then he heard the screaming.

It was muffled at first, but then one of the alarm runners threw open the basement door and yelled:

"Code 10! *Hide!* Code 10!"

The door slammed shut.

He felt cold sweat pop out on his spine like a hundred angry, itchy bees; more than anything else, Jonah was afraid of Novo Mundum being taken away from him. He was finally *safe* in a place where his interests and intelligence would help out—not get him drafted into the Army Corps of Engineers.

Jonah heard the footsteps running away, more doors opening, more yelling, then multiple footsteps and doors as the panic spread.

Code 10. They were being invaded by ground— probably from the pass in the hills to the south of them. Code 10: *hide.*

When they'd all first arrived at N.M., one of the first things they'd done was attend a security seminar. Frank had shown them maps—between two fast rivers and surrounded by pine forest, the old Greenwich College grounds that had become Novo Mundum were almost impossible to notice, much less invade. In the evacuation of the Big Empty and the chaos of the post-7 years, no one would notice or care about the small liberal arts college. There were no major repositories of gas or propane for the government to appropriate, no major cities nearby for soldiers to carefully sweep.

And the only way to get to it by land was from the base of the peninsula on which it was built, the bottom of the delta formed by the two rivers. And *that* route, the broad, paved road that cut through the woods and must have looked mighty impressive to parents driving their kids up their freshman year, had been carefully destroyed, made to look like something either natural or the work of the renegade survivalist group the Slash. Even if soldiers found out about Novo Mundum, they would have to make their way through the woods and over huge gray rocks—with old fraternity logos spray-painted on them—and there were many, *many* trip wires along the way to alert Novo Mundum to their presence.

It was as safe as you could be in a world like this. And within it, the carefully guarded research lab was even safer—Dr. Slattery and his research were all that protected them from future viruses.

Code 10: Make no noise. Make the place look abandoned.

More muffled yells.

When Mom and Dad yelled, you couldn't fix it. You just stayed out of the way until it was all over. Footsteps pounded overhead as people rushed to their assigned hideouts. Jonah dropped to his feet and crawled under the pipes into the farthest, darkest corner he could find. *They won't find me. They'll* never *find me here.*

He clutched the wrench to his chest, closed his eyes, and waited for it to be over.

THREE

THE CHILDREN WERE THE FIRST TO NOTICE THE ALARM—THE LOW, vibrating noise that sounded like someone had turned the bass up way too high. A traditional siren would have alerted whoever was invading that there was a community here, entrenched and prepared. The first time she felt it, Keely—L.A. girl that she was—thought it was an earthquake.

"Miss Gilmore?" one of the boys asked nervously.

"Come on," Keely said as calmly as she could. "Inside."

It was such a beautiful day that Keely had held her class outside, on the small lawn next to what was once the English wing. It was a little hard on the easily distractible eight-year-olds, who would rather have picked at the grass and watched the puffy clouds than learn fractions. But Keely had always imagined college this way: the poetry professor taking the class outside on a particularly fine day to better emphasize the vitality of life, maybe during a lecture on Blake or something. . . .

As wonderful as Novo Mundum was, though, even *it* wasn't completely free of the reality of the world of Strain 7.

The little kids rose, taking their books, as serious and nervous as if it was a fire drill. They headed back toward the building, where there was already a guard stationed outside the door, gesturing with his gun for people to move faster.

"Code ten," he shouted. "This is *not* a drill. Code ten, people. Move it!"

Keely's wards saw the adults running and panicked, beginning to run themselves.

"Careful!" Keely said, trying to herd them before her like ducklings. The guard was talking on his radio and didn't look happy.

She suddenly thought of Amber, the girl she'd brought to Novo Mundum with her, her traveling companion across the Big Empty and now her roommate. Amber was pregnant and easily winded now. Where was she? In the fields? In the gardens? *Can she make it to a basement all right?*

All of the children were almost in when Olivia tripped over the lintel, falling flat on her face and crying. People began piling up behind her, trying to get in.

Keely ducked between them and scooped Olivia up in her arms, following the other children into the building's basement. She dismissed her thoughts about Amber; she was a street-smart kid who could handle herself, right? Keely had other people to worry about right now.

FOUR

"NEGATIVE," FINCH SAID, HANDING MICHAEL HIS RIFLE. "WE do *not* take them out. There are too many of them. If an entire platoon disappears, it will definitely raise suspicions. Plan B."

He took off his headset and gave that to Gabe.

Michael felt his heart sink. He'd expected any one of a number of violent, dangerous, and bloody outcomes to the soldiers' arrival; this wasn't one of them, and somehow it was worse. *Once again I can't do anything.* "Plan B" meant that one of them stripped himself of anything that could connect him to Novo Mundum and wandered out to meet the soldiers, claiming that he was lost or had been attacked by the Slash. Once the soldiers bought the story, he would lead them away from the area. As an ex–U.S. soldier, Finch could easily talk the talk and would probably be immediately accepted by them.

Although he wasn't actually sacrificing his *life,* Finch would be as good as dead to Michael and Gabe and Novo Mundum. Even if he managed to eventually get away from the soldiers, after he was sent to a new town or whatever, he would never be able to return. It was too much of a security risk.

The thought of Finch voluntarily leaving Novo Mundum forever suddenly made Michael choke up, but he swallowed it back and put on a brave face.

"How did they find us?" Gabe wondered. "It sounds like they *knew* we were here. How did they get past the two guards on the road?"

"I don't think they came from the road," Finch said tonelessly. "I think they found another route. Otherwise we would have heard of them earlier." He stood at attention, done with his disarming.

"How did they even know we were here?" Michael asked, still wanting to know how it was possible, not wanting to say good-bye.

Finch looked Michael in the eyes, his blue eyes cold and dead. As if he was already gone.

"Someone must have told them. Someone *also* must have told them to avoid the road. . . ."

They heard it then: the actual sound of other boots crushing the autumn leaves, the crackle of radios not their own.

"Take off," Gabe hissed. "They're coming!"

"Keep your eyes open," Finch said quickly, one hand on the fence. "Someone here still has a connection to the outside. An *informant . . .*"

And with that, he vaulted over the chain-link fence that in the past had protected the old college from local vandals and the occasional coyote in their garbage.

On the other side, Finch saluted one more time and was gone.

FIVE

LIZA HUDDLED IN THE BASEMENT SPIDER HOLE WITH HER father. Uncle Frank would be out and about, giving orders and making sure everyone was good and hidden. Dr. Slattery, though, the real leader of Novo Mundum, was too important to their future to risk. He was holding one of his carefully rationed cigarettes, playing with it in his fingers and occasionally smelling it.

Liza hugged her knees to her chest. She had overheard the communications officer radioing Michael's patrol. His was closest to the break-in point; they were the ones who'd been told to go in and investigate. He shouldn't have gone on duty with the more experienced guards—but Michael had insisted. He wanted to be useful to Novo Mundum, in the best way he could, immediately. And he hadn't been here more than a month!

"Dad," she said as calmly as she could, "you know that Michael was into security systems with his father?"

"The one from the new group? The boy out with Finch and Gabe?"

"Yes, Daddy. That one. When this is over, you should totally talk to him about improving our defenses."

"That sounds like a good idea."

"He's had some *great* ideas for improving our defenses—things he and his dad were doing for people in Washington."

"I said I would talk to him."

"What if he *dies?*" Liza said, biting her lip and grabbing the bottom of her shirt, pulling at it.

"Liza," her father said casually—which was already a warning; nothing Dr. Slattery ever said or did was casual—"is there something else you want to tell me about Michael?"

The first time she'd set eyes on him at the boat dock, Liza had fallen for Michael. He had such an intense, serious look about him—coupled with his perfect, thick blond hair and strong jaw, he was a *very determined* Prince Charming. They ate together all the time now, and went on walks, and stayed up late at night watching the stars and talking about Novo Mundum.

And sometimes not so much with the talking.

"No," she said, trying to sound like she meant it.

Her father was as overprotective with her as he was with N.M.—before Strain 7 she hadn't been allowed to go anywhere near the dorms or college boys, not even the "nice" ones he invited over for Thanksgiving who couldn't afford to fly home. In the two years since Greenwich College had become Novo Mundum, she had been very careful about not upsetting him.

Dr. Slattery looked at her and lowered his eyebrows slightly, the closest he ever came to a frown with her. His gaze was transfixing, though, and she knew she wouldn't be able to avoid what came out next.

Then there was a coded tap on the trapdoor. *Saved by the bell!* Her father undid all of the latches and Ellen helped pull it open from above.

"All clear, sir," she said, putting a hand down to help him up. "Alert is over. But we lost one to the enemy."

"NO!" Liza cried, scrambling over her dad and forcing her way up through the trapdoor. "Who is it? It's not Michael, is it?"

Captain Ellen Tabori looked her over coolly, unsure whether to answer to her or her dad. Ellen was only two years older than Liza was but treated her like a child—worse, a civilian.

"We don't know who it was," she said gently, resting her hand on her gun. "They had orders to keep radio silence until the immediate situation was resolved. Gabe radioed once that plan B worked but that the remaining two would shadow the enemy to the border. They should be returning soon. No more trip wires have been set off, and Kerry in the clock tower reported five people moving in formation onto the lower road."

Liza nodded bravely, but the most important piece of information was missing: *Who was it they'd lost?*

SIX

"ONE LOST . . ."

News spread like wildfire in Novo Mundum. In a community of fifteen hundred, you couldn't trip without everyone talking about it the next day.

Amber felt a detached sorrow for whomever it was who was "down" or "lost" or whatever the military jargon said. But the alert was over and they were safe, and she was back in the greenhouse again, tending to her plants.

Not in a *million years* would she ever have imagined herself fiddling with dirt and seeds; if it weren't for the fact that she was pregnant, she bet that they would have assigned her to something more tactical—like spying or bringing back supplies or something. She was good at things like that. Stealing was her life.

Originally she was just glad they'd given her something to do. All the people in the group who hadn't been contacted directly by N.M. were nervous about their acceptance: Michael, Diego, and her.

"Who are you?" the robed girl had said in surprise on seeing the three unexpected travelers. She held a strange thing, a knife or something tied to the end of her staff, and her companion readied his as well.

"They helped us get here," Keely said immediately, spreading out her hands in supplication. "We couldn't have made it without them."

The girl had frowned. "Dr. Slattery must hear about this."

And they had been marched along, somewhere between escorted dignitaries and prisoners. Amber was exhausted and her stomach was still in the morning sickness stage then; somewhere along the path she had to lean over and retch. Not having eaten in the last day, all that came out was acrid bile.

"Are you okay?" the boy had asked.

"I'm *pregnant,* you dipshit!" Amber had snapped without thinking. Immediately she'd regretted her big mouth, amazed at how easily the secret had slipped out. The boy had looked taken aback for a second, but strangely enough his face brightened, like her news was a pleasant surprise or something.

They were marched through the woods to the campus itself, which was so pretty and perfect and quaint it looked like one of those shots of a fake university on a TV show. Ridiculously old and beautiful buildings, surrounded by newer tents and sheds huddled up to them like chicks around a mother hen. Green grass, silvery clouds, gently rolling hills, and beyond, the university, fields of golden wheat or something. Amber's heart stopped—it was like the Garden of Eden or heaven.

She was overcome with *want*. A want greater than she had ever had before—this was a perfect and beautiful and safe place left in the world. She *had* to live here and raise her baby here.

When they were herded into a room to meet Dr. Slattery, Amber felt another emotion unusual for her: something a little akin to awe. He looked so smart and kindly and spoke so evenly, like a TV dad. He didn't seem to be as upset as his two flunkies were about their presence and asked them gentle questions about their backgrounds and who they were.

Michael was just the sort of suck-up, yes-man ideas guy people in small communities liked, and Diego, though he was injured, knew far more about living off the land and the woods than any of the ex-academics there.

But Amber? She was a thief and a runaway and never really went to school even before Strain 7. . . .

And then . . . Dr. Slattery was *impressed* with the whole stealing Faith Stank's identity thing and helping Keely get here. He called her *resourceful* and *street-smart*. When the boy with the knife-stick told him about her condition, Dr. Slattery was *thrilled*. Like she had just brought them the winning lottery ticket or something. He said something about viable populations and increasing the gene pool . . . but he and everyone else there were just thrilled and treated her like a queen.

And queens, apparently, did not go on patrol or bring back supplies.

At first Amber objected to the job; she had never been in a greenhouse before and found it hot, humid, close, and unpleasant. Though it was cool seeing all the weird plants people at Greenwich College studied or did research on. The orchids were the coolest, but unfortunately many of them had to be gotten rid of to make room for the crops that kept Novo Mundum going through the winter.

Like the radishes Amber was working on.

She couldn't believe it, looking at the neat little row of leafy green fountains that stretched across the troughs. Just a few weeks ago, when she'd first arrived, the other gardeners had showed her how to plant the seeds and keep them moist. And now—she pulled one up delicately, revealing a shiny red globe, as perfect as anything you could buy at the supermarket.

Me. I did this, she said to herself, spinning it around in wonder. *From seed to salad.*

"Whoa. You okay, Amber?" Duke asked as he came around an aisle and saw her.

"Yeah, it's just—" She didn't know how to explain it. "I made a radish," she said lamely.

He smiled, but not unkindly. "Quite a triumph for a city girl. You're really doing an amazing job here—I'm glad they assigned you to us."

"I'm just grateful to be here," Amber murmured, hating how dumb it sounded. But it was true. She would have scrubbed toilets to stay.

"Security meeting tonight—that's what I came by to tell you. Sort of a recap on how we did today and what we can do next time. Seven o'clock in the drama auditorium. Tell Cindy if you see her."

The drama *auditorium*? As Duke wandered off, Amber thought about this. It sounded like just about half of Novo Mundum would be there. So far she had only seen that bastard father of her baby, Carter, in passing, from a distance, and she wasn't even sure he knew she was there. It was certainly an opportunity to confront him. . . .

Then her stomach did something it had never done before.

A weird, fluttery movement from inside. Not hunger. Not upset. Lower.

"Is that you, Junior?" Amber whispered, putting her hand to her belly. There was another flutter, and she could feel it with her fingers this time. The hand with the forgotten radish fell to her side, leaves gently brushing against her skin.

SEVEN

"ONE LOST? WHICH ONE?" DIEGO ASKED ANXIOUSLY AS IRENE helped him back to his dorm.

"I don't know," Irene said, holding his arm while trying not to look like she was . . . well, holding his arm. The wound should have been healing fine on its own now, but he hadn't used that leg in days. It was much weaker than it should have been.

"Man, I hope it wasn't Michael. Isn't it crazy how he's been since we got here? So . . . together. But cool about it."

"Yeah. Kind of like a Slattery-in-training," Irene said, smiling gently. "I'm sure it wasn't him."

"Hey, Diego!" A girl came running up to him, small and pretty. But then again, all the girls in Novo

Mundum were pretty, as far as Diego was concerned. Happiness had a way of doing that to people. He supposed that the families and younger siblings and male members of Novo Mundum were just as relaxed and gorgeous—but he, uh, didn't really notice them. "I was supposed to give you these, before the alert." She handed him a pile of books, tied up in an old-fashioned satchel so he could carry them when he was by himself on his crutches. "Dr. Slattery was afraid you might get bored in between your sessions. He thought you might like these."

There was a careful selection of different genres—science fiction, mystery, Western, and a light comedy of some sort.

"Wow, thanks."

"Not a worry," she said, giving him a last smile before dancing off.

Not a worry was the unofficial motto of Novo Mundum. While the vibe definitely had some hippie overtones—Diego and Jonah had discussed whether or not free love was among those things—it was more of a wish for the future. Novo Mundum: No More Worries.

"That was really thoughtful of him," Irene said, impressed.

"Yeah. I'll bet he's got a zillion better things to do running this place. But . . . that's just the kind of guy he is." Diego frowned.

"What's wrong?" Irene asked, concerned.

"I wish I could help more," he said, shaking the books in frustration. "You know, I was kind of scared they wouldn't let me join because I wasn't one of you specially chosen brainiacs—but if worst came to worst, as long as my leg healed, I'd be fine back out on my own again. Now . . ." He gestured around the campus. They were on the main walking road that students would have taken to class at one time, beautifully landscaped between the white marble-faced buildings and lawns. Some of the greenery was now partly built over with makeshift sheds and tents, and some had been converted into fields. Greenwich had been a small school, and they were just about maxing out its capacity. But it didn't look like a shantytown. Everybody was recovering from the alert, back at their jobs, happy and industrious—and *clean,* which was more than Diego could say about any of the people he and his nonnie used to see in the years after the virus hit. People waved to each other, stopping to talk, and someone played a guitar.

"I want to *help,*" he finished, shaking his head. "I'm still not completely into this whole communal living thing, but it's kind of nice seeing people again. At least I want to be able to repay Dr. S. and everyone for the medical attention they're giving me. Everyone works here—I want to work too. I want to be part of that. I'm *sick* of being a useless patient."

"I know. It's going to be just a little longer," she promised.

And when she said that and looked at him so seriously with her black eyes, Diego couldn't help but believe her.

If nothing else, at least his injury meant he got to spend more time with Irene.

EIGHT

"WHAT ARE YOU DOING DOWN HERE?" DR. SLATTERY ASKED Jonah with light humor as he and Liza and Captain Tabori passed through the rest of the basement on their way out. Liza almost tapped her foot with impatience but didn't want to appear weak in front of Ellen. She wished she could be more like her dad, who was calm and collected at every moment. And *personable.* People worshiped him for that.

Jonah brushed some cobwebs out of his short black hair, a little embarrassed.

"When the alarm came, I was already down here, sir. Working on the pipes. I figured I would just stay here since it's a basement and out of the way and all."

"Good thinking, staying out of the way of everyone

else. But please, call me Dr. Slattery. Everyone else does."

"Yes, si—uh, Dr. Slattery."

"Now come on, let's see what messes we have to clean up." He put an arm each behind Liza and Jonah and ushered them upstairs behind the captain, like they were just going up for a glass of lemonade or something else equally innocuous. *While Michael could be lying dead somewhere.* When Liza went first, no one said anything.

Outside, a crowd had gathered around a pair of people—Gabe and *Michael,* walking determinedly up the path.

"Michael!" Liza yelled, running up to him and hugging him. Though he seemed a little dazed and distracted, he was definitely receptive, putting his arms back around her and holding tightly before letting go. With no fear about how it might look to everyone else.

It wasn't *exactly* the way Liza wanted to introduce her new boyfriend to her dad, but he was alive and well, and that was enough. She sneaked a look over; her father was nodding, as if this was exactly what he expected. Beyond that, there was no expression on his face.

Gabe just looked grim.

"Sir, Finch plan B'ed. We followed them for a klick and they showed no sign at all of interest in returning. I think they bought his story."

"What a brave young man," Dr. Slattery said gravely. "I hope his sacrifice for us doesn't cost him his life as well. I hope he finds peace somewhere in the world outside." Without it even being suggested, everyone bowed their heads for a moment, sending Finch their best wishes. She felt terrible, but Liza also thanked whatever powers that were that it had been Finch and not Michael.

Then Uncle Frank dismissed the two guards reporting to him and came over. "Everyone's fine," he reported. "One little girl has a scraped knee, but that's the only injury. And two cook fires were left on," he added, growling. "It's a good thing my boys stopped them. Otherwise they would have known someone was still here—or the entire place would have burned down. I think we should discuss this at the general security meeting tonight to recap what happened."

Dr. Slattery sighed. "I suppose you're going to tell me that this is exactly what you predicted would happen with our current security procedures."

Uncle Frank just glared at her dad. He was an ex-marine and had kept the jarhead hairstyle, which wasn't really that attractive on his giant, square head. Except for around the mouth a little, Liza once again found it hard to believe that these two were brothers. She took in a breath, ready to tell everyone about Michael's plans.

She didn't have to.

"Dr. Slattery," Michael spoke up. "I don't know if anyone told you, but I used to work with my dad at his security company."

The head of Novo Mundum gave Liza the slightest look, then turned his full attention to him. "Yes, someone mentioned that, I believe. I was just going to get around to talking to you. Before the general meeting tonight, why don't you join me and Frank and Halley and Ellen in my office to discuss this."

Inside, Liza was cheering. Such a small thing, but she knew her dad. He was giving Michael a chance to show off, to do his stuff and prove his worth. That alone meant he liked what he saw.

"You too, Jonah," her dad said, turning back to the silent boy, who was obviously uncertain if he was dismissed or not. His eyes widened with surprise—Dr. Slattery knew his *name?* "You're the closest thing to an engineer we have here except for old Ridley. In an hour, people."

"Yes, sir," Jonah said, forgetting himself.

"Dr. Slattery." Michael reached for the older man as he turned away, without quite touching him. "I want to do everything I can to make sure this never happens again. I *will* do everything I can."

"I'm glad to hear it," Dr. Slattery said. "I think we all are."

NINE

No one seemed to know who the missing patrolman was. One lost, that was all that kept circulating. She didn't want to cause a scene, but Keely had to find out who it was. Michael was on guard duty that morning. . . .

After the all clear she had let her charges go for the day. She probably shouldn't have; they were at the age where they would have to begin to learn that life didn't stop when things like this happened. The whole *point* of Novo Mundum was that people had to rise above the horrible things that were happening around them and keep working toward a better world. Some of the students, like Paula, probably could have handled going back to their studies. But Olivia . . .

There was a small crowd talking excitedly in front of Alumni Hall, where Dr. Slattery's office was. Jonah separated himself from them and headed her way, smiling when he saw her.

"Hey," she said. "Is Michael okay, do you know?"

"Yeah. The one they lost was Finch—and he's not dead, or at least not yet. I don't really understand it, but I guess they had this plan where he pretended he was lost or something and let himself 'get found' by the enemy and bring them out of here."

As he spoke, Michael and Gabe came around from the other side of the research building, avoiding the crowd. They were talking too intently to notice what was going on, even when Keely waved. She gave up and finally ran after them, Jonah following.

"You made it back, soldier boy!" she blurted.

Michael spun around, obviously still revved up from the encounter in the woods. She gave him a friendly hug. "I'm so glad you're okay."

"Jesus," Gabe swore. "You got girls hanging all over you. How about *me*, Gilmore? I'm okay too, you know." He presented his arms wide and Keely laughed, chucking him on the shoulder instead.

"Listen, I was just talking to Gabriel about this," Michael said, serious. "You should hear this too, Jonah." He beckoned him to come closer. "Right before he left us, Finch said something about the enemy being *told* that we were here and how to get here safely."

"He was kind of cryptic," Gabe added, shrugging.

"How would they know that?" Jonah asked. "Satellite or something?"

Michael shook his head. "That's not what he seemed to be saying. He was telling us that there's a spy in Novo Mundum."

TEN

LIZA WALKED CAREFULLY WITH THE TWO MUGS OF COFFEE—
one for Gabe, one for Michael. The real stuff, not
instant cut with chicory, which they were all going to
have to accustom themselves to soon. She kept her eye
on the sidewalk, stepping gently. When she looked up to
make sure she was headed in the right direction, she
saw Keely hugging Michael.

Liza stopped, unable to tear her eyes away, unwill-
ing to risk spilling the hot beverage in her hands. Keely
was radiant with the joy at Michael being alive—and
she very specifically did *not* hug Gabe. Michael's face
turned serious and the three—no, four of them; Jonah
was there too—lowered their heads and started talking,
Keely nodding and looking worried. If only Keely wasn't

quite so pretty—even from a distance her perfectly smooth sandy blond hair gleamed in the sun, and Liza could imagine her striking blue eyes narrowing in concentration as she focused on Michael's words.

What was Michael telling her that he hadn't told Liza?

Biting back disappointment, she told herself that the two friends weren't romantically interested in each other, no matter how shiny Keely's hair was. *Obviously,* otherwise they would have hooked up before getting to Novo Mundum. Otherwise Michael wouldn't have been into Liza so deeply and so quickly.

The thing was, if Keely just flat-out liked Michael, Liza could have been righteously jealous. But the relationship the two *actually* had was somehow worse: they were close friends who had bonded over their trials getting to Novo Mundum, something Liza hadn't been part of. She *wanted* that kind of depth and trust—*and* Michael as her boyfriend. He never talked with her like that, all seriously, in that almost shorthand the group who had come in from Clearwater used.

She strode forward, determined to change things.

"Here, Gabe," she said, carefully handing his mug over first, not to appear overanxious. "Michael. Without sugar or milk." She smiled.

"Freak," Gabe muttered.

"Hey, Liza." Keely smiled warmly at her, no trace of anything but friendliness. This just unnerved her further—shouldn't Keely be just a *little* bit threatened by her? She *was* the girlfriend in between their friendship, after all. It was like Liza wasn't even an issue.

"You're the best, Liza," Gabe added.

No one said anything about what they had just been discussing. They had obviously dropped it when she appeared.

She just smiled back. "Enjoy—I'll see you guys later."

"Are you going back to the dorms? I'll walk with you," Keely said, waving to the three boys.

"No—I have to go see my uncle Frank," Liza stuttered.

But now that she thought about it, it wasn't such a bad idea. . . .

"Okay, see you." And the other girl left, as easily as she had come.

It was kind of irritating how nice Keely was—it just made that anxious feeling in Liza's stomach even worse, because how could she resent someone so nice? Liza watched her go, then went into Alumni Hall. The guards ignored her as she waltzed in. Uncle Frank's office was small, probably an adjunct professor's or something originally; he claimed he didn't need space to do paperwork now that there wasn't a lot of paper left. His place was in the "situation room," in security and information, he always said.

But he was at his old-fashioned wooden desk now, frowning at a book about electrified fencing for farms and livestock. The same one he had been studying for weeks. He *never* stopped arguing with his brother about how defenseless Novo Mundum was, without even a real perimeter wall or moat or whatever.

"Kitten," he said, putting the book down, his face softening. He was hard with everyone else—even his own brother—but Liza was his pride and joy, almost as if *he* was her father. Understandable, since he had no kids of his own. "What can I do for you?"

"I was thinking about coming to the meeting with you guys. I think I should learn more about security around here," she said, putting on her best serious face.

Uncle Frank sighed. "I don't know if that's a good idea. You've never been interested before—and I'm *sure* a certain new member of our little community has nothing to do with it." He raised his eyebrows at her.

While her dad was concerned with Novo Mundum and the philosophy of the human condition—and therefore always distracted—Uncle Frank's full-time job was keeping tabs on everything and everyone. He had no illusions about her and Michael's relationship—and had been nice enough not to burden her father with the information. So far.

". . . and don't want to have to keep stopping to answer your questions," he finished. She hadn't really heard what came before.

"I won't ask any. *Promise.*"

"Liza, this is foolishness. You have your place here, and your future probably doesn't include maintaining our security."

"Because I'm a *girl?*" she demanded, stomping her foot.

"You know that's not how I feel. Ellen and Halley will be at the meeting tonight."

The two locked eyes for a moment, his hard gray-blue and hers soft brown.

He backed down first.

"I suppose you're going to ask your dad if I say no," the ex-marine said, resigned.

"I would *never* do that to you, Uncle Frank!" Liza said with a twinkle in her eyes.

"Hmmph." He picked up his book again.

"Thank you, Uncle Frank!" she called, practically skipping out.

This was perfect. Not only would she learn what the four had been talking about and get in on the inside, but she would be there to support Michael and his ideas.

It was a win-win situation.

ELEVEN

JONAH COULDN'T BELIEVE HE WAS BEING ALLOWED TO SIT IN ON this meeting—everyone else there was so important. Dr. Slattery, Frank, Ridley . . . command, security, and operations. Ellen *looked* like a soldier, pretty with her pixie-cut black hair but a hardness to her face that made you instantly trust her with your life. Halley managed a lot of the resources of the community; as an ex–movie production coordinator, everything went smoothly under her hands. Liza was there, which only made sense, being Dr. Slattery's daughter. And Michael and Gabe, who had been there when Finch had to go.

Michael would be here anyway. He's probably going to be running this place someday, Jonah thought with a wry grin.

They sat around a table—Uncle Frank was sitting ramrod straight, Dr. Slattery relaxed, back in his chair, pushed away from the table a little. Like he was just moderating a panel of equals. Like he wasn't the head honcho. Somehow Jonah couldn't see Michael doing that with his style of leadership. His was to hand things down from the top; Dr. Slattery inspired you from the ground up.

"I want to start this off by once again thanking Finch," the doctor said. "This is only the second time we've ever had to use plan B. He did us a great honor by sacrificing himself for us. We'll miss him—*I'll* miss him. He was a great resource, a great soldier, and an outstanding member of the community. . . ."

"That's why he chose to go," Jonah said before he could stop himself. "He knew that the needs of the many outweigh the needs of the few or the one. He knew that sometimes sacrifices have to be made by the individual to protect the group."

Everyone nodded. He had their attention, their ears. It was amazing.

"Michael here," Jonah continued, pointing at him, "has some *great* ideas for increasing our defenses. Including an electric fence he says would be really easy to set up—strong enough to stun or even kill intruders. I'm sorry about Finch, but with Michael's new plans this may never happen again. Novo Mundum needs better security *now,* and I'm willing to do whatever it takes to get it up, even if it means working around the clock, night and day."

"If we're talking about rejiggering the current fence and gate system to be electrified," Ridley said with a snort, "you *will* be working night and day."

"Fine by me," Jonah responded easily. He'd never been afraid of hard work, and now more than ever—when all the work he did had a real purpose—it just felt good to be useful.

TWELVE

MICHAEL TRIED NOT TO SMILE AT RIDLEY'S CYNICISM. THE OLD man had been in charge of maintenance back when the campus was still Greenwich College and had taken the changes more in stride than most of the remaining academics and staff.

And except for the accent, he also bore a more than passing resemblance to Groundskeeper Willy from *The Simpsons,* which made his gruffness hard to take without giggling.

"I'm glad you decided to come to this meeting," Dr. Slattery said to Jonah. "I *knew* you would be an inspiration."

Jonah fairly glowed with the compliment, his dark skin going rosy on his cheeks. But he still looked at

Michael nervously—he *really* wanted this to work. Michael would have to remember to thank Jonah later for his support.

Liza gave him a wink and smile, quick so no one else in the room would catch it, not even her hawk-eyed uncle. While Michael basked in her attention, her presence there also made him a little nervous. Dr. Slattery really was as great as everyone said at Novo Mundum, but he was still her father. He and his brother could make a mean pair of chaperones if they took a dislike to his relationship with Liza.

"I was just trying to familiarize myself with the whole concept," Frank said, almost as if he guessed Michael was thinking about him, "as it pertains to keeping cows in and bears out of pastures. But those types of fences have to be built from the ground up—what do we do, build a whole 'nother ring around the campus's current fencing?"

"And can't those just be cut with rubber-handled wire cutters?" Ellen asked. "Seems to me if a MacCauley soldier came upon a seven-foot electrified fence with barbed wire at the top, they'd become suspicious pretty damn fast—like they did with that other colony."

"We would know as soon they touched it. *Instantly,*" Michael said. "An alarm would go off, and if it was a sophisticated enough system, it would let us know *exactly* where the voltage drop occurred."

"Is there any way we can hide the electrified elements?" Halley asked. She looked like a middle-aged housewife, with too much hair piled on the top of her head and too many pounds filling out her voluminous clothes. But her brown eyes were bright with intelligence, and though she didn't speak much, when she did, it was worth listening to.

"Absolutely," Michael said, looking to Dr. Slattery before continuing. The older man nodded, one eyebrow raised and an intrigued look on his face. "What I suggest is several concentric rings of wire—if we have enough—each no more than six inches off the ground. Most people aren't looking at their feet or their shins when they walk, so we'll have the element of surprise— at least the first time."

"Can it be strong enough to *kill?*" Frank asked. Other people at the meeting shifted nervously in their chairs.

Michael tried to keep the shock out of his voice. He understood where Frank was coming from—they really were in a life-or-death situation out here in the Big Empty. He knew that more than anyone after everything he'd gone through on his way here. "Yes, if we can provide a continuous flow of five thousand volts. To stun we would just need pulses—once a second or so."

"Doesn't an electric fence require, uh, *electricity?*" Ridley drawled. "Something we don't have in too much supply here?"

"That's one good reason to use the stun system," Michael continued. He glanced nervously back at Dr. Slattery, but the man just motioned for him to continue, to take the floor. "All we'd need is a twelve-volt battery, which could be charged by the AC you have working here or DC directly from a solar panel. Then we'd need a—well, it gets complicated, but a sort of electronic 'funnel' that would increase the voltage to five thousand volts. Also, I was thinking that we could have it only turn itself on if someone sets off the trip wires and pressure plates you already have installed as a warning system."

"That sounds like an excellent plan," Dr. Slattery decided. "Can we implement it?"

"Yeah, we have enough wire and I can get a twelve-volt battery, but with the other stuff and whatever you need to actually make it live, I don't know," Ridley said, sucking one of his back teeth. "That sounds like it needs to be controlled by a computer or something."

"Some of the more intricate electric fences for the big agribusiness farms are run by a central computer," Frank said. "If we can get the right interface and software, I don't see it being a problem. Something like x10, but deadlier." He leaned forward, excited.

"Where would we get that stuff?" Ridley demanded.

Event though he was now sort of out of the conversation, Michael was pleased. These men—*men,* as in *grown-ups*—were taking his idea and flying with it. He traded another smile with Liza, who was beaming.

"Well, it's rather serendipitous, isn't it?" Dr. Slattery said, leaning forward. "I'll bet we can get it the same place we can get those locator disks I've been talking so much about, from that warehouse in St. Louis."

"If we had those GPS locator disks with us now, we'd be able to wait until it was safe and then track down Finch and rescue him," Gabe said, a little sadly.

Michael's father had mentioned the locator chips several times over the past year. The MacCauley government was all about keeping the Global Positioning System satellites in working order, with engineers manning the terrestrial controls. Even before Strain 7 hit, people were already having them put on pet collars and sometimes even their children. The Whereify was an armband for kids that had a locator chip built in. It was kind of creepy, though—parents could use a control to remotely lock the handcuff-like watch so it couldn't be taken off.

But now, with less than half of the population of the United States left, it wasn't insane that people wanted to do a better job of keeping track of those who remained. Michael's dad had actually done a job for one paranoid, rich old man who, terrified of losing anyone else, had wanted to "chip" everyone in his family who had survived.

"I've seen those disks," Michael spoke up. "They work really well. Because they link to a satellite, we wouldn't 'lose signal'—Finch could be taken to Mexico and we'd still know where he was."

"Wouldn't we need to hack into it? The government satellite, I mean?" Halley asked.

"Uh, no," Michael said as delicately as he could. She had obviously worked on one too many bad spy movies—or was a lot less intelligent than he'd originally thought. "It doesn't really work like that. I mean, it's the GPS *device* that triangulates a locator disk's position from several satellites' signals. . . ." He looked at all the blank faces staring at him, all except for that of Frank, who nodded. "Uh, basically, no," Michael added. "There is no satellite hacking. Trust me on this one."

Michael hesitated. He didn't want to jeopardize what seemed to be the good thing he had going, but he had to ask. He couldn't stop himself.

"Dr. Slattery?" he said politely. Liza shot him a look, hearing his tone and definitely warning him. "I don't mean to be rude, but *why* the GPS disks? Everyone's right here, except for occasional incidents like Finch. . . ."

"Actually, everyone's *not* here," Dr. Slattery responded with a chuckle, not unkindly. "But you didn't realize that because you came to us of your own accord. We have operatives all over the country who help choose new members and send them our way. A girl named Ineo bravely volunteered to leave us and return to her hometown in L.A.—she's the one who told your friend Keely how to get here. We have no way of keeping track of our 'field operatives' right now, since we have a policy of no or limited direct contact while they're out there."

That made perfect sense, of course. He saw Liza relaxing. Novo Mundum was even better organized than he thought—he hadn't realized how actively they recruited people. Keely never spoke about it much; maybe she was afraid it would embarrass him, not having been chosen. "Yes, sir. I get it now."

"So," Slattery said, leaning forward and tapping on the table with his index finger. "I think we should initiate a mission to go to the warehouse in St. Louis and retrieve the equipment needed for these two projects. It's kismet."

"I'll go," Michael and Gabe said, both volunteering at the same time.

Dr. Slattery laughed. "Of course you will. Michael, we need you to choose the right stuff to, uh, 'borrow.'"

"I think I might even know that warehouse," Michael said, thinking about it. "Securasystems, one of my dad's old competitors, had its HQ in St. Louis. I'll bet it's theirs."

"Excellent! And Gabe, I think your going as guard would be a fitting memorial to your brother at arms."

"Yes, sir."

Frank cleared his throat. "We'll load one of the light jeeps onto a raft to get it to old Rift Valley Road. From there you can make your way to I-70—shouldn't take you more than half a day to get there. We'll give you an extra tank of gas—and a few empty ones. Part of your mission will be to fill 'em up."

"Sir, two's company . . ." Ellen said quietly.

"And three's a team," Dr. Slattery finished, nodding. The first time he'd heard the saying, Michael had thought it was a little weird. But almost everything at Novo Mundum was done in teams of three if it required more than one person. It kind of made sense, though: everyone had lost too many people to the virus, and it was definitely comforting to have a couple of people around—or at least available—at all times. "Who will be your third?"

"Can't give you anyone from security," Frank said. "With Finch gone, we have even fewer patrols."

It didn't matter. Michael knew the *perfect* person. Someone he worked easily with. Someone Gabe also liked. Someone who was smart, could handle herself well, and didn't go to pieces. Someone who could *drive*—since he couldn't and Gabe shouldn't have to do all of it himself.

"I know the perfect girl for the job," he said. Liza looked over at him, smiling. Frank sucked in a deep breath, worried. "Keely Gilmore."

Frank breathed a sigh of relief.

THIRTEEN

Liza didn't have a chance to talk to Michael until dinner. After the meeting he was too busy talking excitedly with Gabe about the details of their trip. After *that* Ellen took them into command central to show them the giant map of Missouri on the wall with all the little flags on it, different colors indicating different resources or presumed dangers. Once everyone had the GPS disks, she said, they could build much more accurate maps and keep better track of people on missions.

He had the nerve to kiss Liza—distractedly—good-bye on the cheek when she left.

"It would be *great* to show people during orientation." Her father was still talking about it hours later. He and his brother were walking toward the research lab.

"Come on, Frank. Even *you* have to see that. Imagine, everyone being tracked on the computer screen, all of the little dots moving, working, resting. . . . When you join us at Novo Mundum, you're joining a community of wholeness. A *constellation,* a *system* of togetherness."

"Looks more like a damn video game. Like Civilization or something."

"Even better! These kids can relate to that. . . ."

He didn't even see his own daughter as she passed him. *Figures.* Uncle Frank nodded at her and gave her a look that quite clearly said, "It's for the best, honey." Whatever. At least her meal group this week put her together with Michael and none of the others he had arrived with, except for Diego. She ran the rest of the way to dining hall B, shivering in the cool night air.

He was already sitting at their table, in the far corner of the happy, warm, and noisy hall, leaning over and talking to Geri, a girl from Russia originally—Rhode Island more recently. She was blond and willowy—but a little *too* thin and weird to make her someone to be jealous of. Liza walked in slowly, trying not to look overanxious.

"Hey, Liza!" Michael saw her as she approached and leaned over the table to kiss her hello. He didn't even realize anything was wrong.

"Hey." She sat primly down. "What's on the menu tonight?"

"Beef stew with some actual beef in it," Geri answered as one of their other meal group members came around and began to dish it out into their bowls.

"And some sort of whole-rye-cracker-bread thing they're experimenting with." She held her hand over her own bowl to prevent anything from being poured in.

"You're Going Without *again?*" Michael asked. "That's two times this week."

"Once for putting some food by," Geri said, blushing, trying not to be the center of attention, "and once for Amber and Deirdre and Lotetia and their, uh, you know." She patted her stomach.

"You're an example for us all," Diego said, completely honestly—while slurping down his stew.

Liza opened her mouth to start in on Michael, but then it was the Moment of Silence, when everyone remembered who was lost to Strain 7, gave thanks they were here now, and promised to change the future.

"Michael," she pleaded as soon as it was over and social murmurs and dishware clinking slowly banished the silence. "What were you thinking?"

He gave her a blank look. "When?"

"Don't you care about me? About *us?*" She didn't mean to make it sound so hissed, but she really didn't want anyone else to hear. There were some people at N.M. who thought *every*thing was up for discussion.

"Liza," he said with genuine incomprehension, his brown eyes looking—as they so rarely did—soft and confused. "What are you talking about?"

"Why did you decide to take Keely along and not me?" she whispered while passing the bowl of bread things to Uche.

"Uh," Michael said, looking around him as if for an

answer, but even Geri found something interesting to stare at in her empty bowl. "Uh," he said again. "What?"

"You didn't even *think* of me, did you?" Liza hissed.

"Well, no," he finally said, a little exasperated. "You've never been out there—you've been here since *before* Strain 7, safe and sheltered. Keely and Amber found their way by themselves even when everything got all screwed up. Frankly, as much as she's kind of a pain, Amber would even be better—but you know, the baby. Jonah's busy with stuff around here; so is Irene, and Diego's injured."

The things he said made perfect sense. It only made Liza more frustrated, though: she couldn't even be angry at *him*. Just that he was going without her. And with Keely.

"Well, I could go *with* the three of you," she said, a little petulantly. "I'd be safe with you and could take turns on watch or something."

"Liza." Michael sighed. "There is *no way* I'm asking your dad, the head of Novo Mundum, to let his princess go out with me on a potentially deadly mission."

Liza bristled. *Princess???!*

Michael held up his hand.

"He *just* found out that we were seeing each other, and not really in the best way—the way we should have told him. I wasn't even *asked* to join, Liza—I'm here because of your dad's good graces. I don't want to screw this up. I don't even know what he thinks about me—or us—yet. Let me go out and do this and, when I come back successful, earn his respect."

"It would have been nice to spend some time away together," Liza finally said, trying not to sound pissy, realizing she'd failed.

"This isn't a pleasure trip," Michael said soothingly, reaching over and tucking a loose strand of hair back behind her ear. "It's dangerous. There's the Slash, soldiers—even just finding the damn place. I don't want you hurt."

"You think I can't handle the outside world," she muttered.

"*I* can barely handle the outside world. And look at Diego—he was a survivalist and look what happened to *him*. Uh, no offense."

"None taken," Diego said, a little amused, shifting in his seat to rest his crutches better against the table.

"I guess," Liza agreed gloomily, pouting a little. This was obviously one she really *wasn't* going to win.

FOURTEEN

Michael kissed Liza good-bye after dinner, promising to see her that evening after one more strategy session with Ellen and Frank. Diego waited for him politely a few feet away.

"Girl troubles—*again?*"

"What do you mean *again?* They're all *new* troubles." Michael smiled. "Liza is nothing like Maggie."

"Uh-huh," Diego said neutrally.

"What's that supposed to mean?"

"Nothing at all." He sighed. "I really wish I was going with you."

"I wish you were too. You're a damn good shot."

"Just a few more weeks," Diego growled. "Just a few more and I'll be better. Then I can join you guys and—"

Michael held up his hand. There was some sort of altercation going on at the entrance to the research labs; as they got closer, he saw it was Dr. MacTavish, the community's physician, throwing up her hands and yelling at the security guards.

"What do you *mean,* I can't go in? I'm the only actual *doctor* here!"

"I'm sorry, ma'am—"

"Doctor," she corrected in a steely tone.

"Doctor," the guard said easily. He was from the pre-MacCauley era, as perfect and formal a soldier as you could have guarding the most important building on campus. "These are *Doctor* Slattery's orders. No one off the main committee can go in without his direct approval."

The two faced off, Dr. MacTavish with her graying heather-colored hair and dark flinty eyes, almost the same height as the decades-younger guard.

"I just want to get some supplies," she finally admitted, relenting. "We're all out of sterile gauze in the infirmary and I *know* they brought cartloads of it back in here last week. Unless they're *researching* how to make mummies, I think we need it more for emergencies."

"That sounds reasonable, Doctor, but I'm afraid you'll still have to bring it up with Dr. Slattery before I can let you in."

"You . . . *military plebeian!*" she spat before spinning on her heels and marching off.

"That was . . . odd," Michael said. While it was rare for any disagreement to reach shouting level at Novo Mundum, among the adults it was unheard of.

"She's a little snappish," Diego said, shrugging as best he could with the crutches under his arms. "They're apprenticing Irene to her since she loves the whole medical thing so much, and she says that MacTavish is under a lot of pressure. You know, no supplies, random electricity. Plus she used to be a dermatologist."

Michael turned and raised his eyebrows.

"Yeah, I know, huh?" Diego chuckled. "And now she's setting limbs and stuff. She's not into this whole communal living thing as much as the others."

"She doesn't *like* Novo Mundum?" Michael asked, surprised.

"I don't think she . . . 'works well with others.' And she doesn't really agree with a lot of what Dr. Slattery says."

Michael frowned. There hadn't been any real accidents or emergencies around the campus for the last couple of weeks—nothing that would require bandages, anyway. Why was she so adamant about getting inside the research facility?

And Dr. MacTavish was so out in the open—to Irene at least—about her feelings. She had no problem screaming at the guard in public. Like someone who was on the edge, just about fed up with everything. He thought about Finch's warning. Someone had let MacCauley's men know the best route into Novo Mundum. . . . Maybe it hadn't been a spy per se, just a malcontent.

He would definitely check up on her as soon as he was back. But in the meantime she needed to be watched.

"Hey, Diego, could you do me a favor?"

"Sure—whatever I can."

"Could you tell Irene to sort of keep an eye on the good doctor?"

"Absolutely, but why?"

"Uh, it's just a hunch. She's obviously kind of trouble—and right before he left us, Finch said he was pretty sure there was a saboteur in our midst."

"You're kidding!" Diego said, whistling. "*Here?* I can't believe it. Everyone seems so . . . happy."

"I know, but there's no way anyone could have even *known* we were here—and the soldiers managed to avoid all of the alarms and trip wires perfectly. Like someone told them the way."

"Huh—well, I'll tell Irene and keep my own eyes peeled too," he promised. Michael knew Diego would do it. He was really desperate to be any sort of help.

"Are you going to the big security meeting tonight?"

"Nah. That's for work groups one, two, and three. I'm in four right now—we're trying to rig spinning wheels out of old bikes."

"Sounds more like Jonah's domain."

"Not since he got drafted into the new Internal Defense Team," Diego said with a sigh. "Tonight it's just me, some tools, and a dozen dedicated would-be weavers. All girls," he added with a wink.

"Yeah, I'm *so sure* you're going to do anything."

Diego grinned. They both knew he was all talk—and all about Irene.

FIFTEEN

IT WAS GETTING DIFFICULT FOR AMBER TO SIT IN ONE POSITION for very long. There was a funny weight on the back of her spine and these days she only had to *think* about water to suddenly have to pee.

Dr. Slattery was on the stage with most of the main committee and Dr. MacTavish and that girl soldier and a few other military types, recapping the near-invasion today and droning on about electric fences, trip wires, increased awareness, heightened security, etc., etc. . . .

There was another flutter in her belly, like goldfish were swimming through. Amber put a hand protectively on it.

Okay, maybe all this stuff isn't such a bad thing.

Novo Mundum was a great place to raise a baby—probably the last great place in America. It *needed* to stay safe. She tried to pay more attention, but it really was deadly boring.

". . . locator devices. Basically like the GPSs mountain bikers and hikers used to use, but these are much smaller," Frank was saying, gripping the sides of the podium like he was going to lean forward and personally reprimand every single one of them. He was almost a cartoon of a jarhead. "These would be worn like a medical bracelet or, more likely, implanted under the skin."

What? Amber suddenly focused. They were going to do *what?* They were going to bury a computer chip in her flesh? Like on the *X-Files* or something?

The old Amber resurfaced for a moment. Who did these people think they were, *tracking* everyone like dogs or cattle or something? She felt a little guilty thinking those thoughts; they had taken her into their little paradise with no questions, welcomed her gladly— but still. This sounded like something MacCauley would cook up.

"No way," she muttered. "I only got room for *one* thing inside me."

"Dr. MacTavish will now explain the procedure, for those of you who feel queasy about the idea. Doctor?"

He ceded the podium. Dr. MacTavish was wearing a white lab coat and *pumps,* as if it were still the old days, as if she were an important doctor far above them instead of just another Mundian. Amber rolled her eyes.

"Basically it's a simple incision on either the thigh or upper arm," the middle-aged woman indicated, pulling back her coat to illustrate. "While it may sting a little, no anesthesia will be needed—topical numbing cream at the most. Those of you who have had subdermal birth control should be familiar with the process. The chip will rest just below the surface of the fatty layer of skin, almost visible and easily removable if it's damaged or needs to be reprogrammed.

"Although," she added dryly, "security here may already exceed what's actually needed when the head of surgery can't get supplies and equipment."

It was said almost as a joke . . . but not. Frank glared at her and Dr. Slattery rolled his eyes, gently amused. *What the hell was that about?* Amber wondered vaguely, losing interest as the doctor began talking again.

Amber looked out over the crowd. This was one of three auditoriums on campus, in what was once the theater department. The seats were velvet covered and comfy, and there were plasterwork scrolls on the walls that were gold in places. Not the sort of place Amber ever would have imagined herself being in. Most of the "green" people in work group two sat together; one was education or something—yeah, there was Keely—and three . . .

Carter.

He was only a few rows behind her and to the left. There were empty seats next to him.

Carter. The whole reason she was here. The jerk

who'd given her a place to stay, gotten her pregnant, and then taken off. She had followed him to New Orleans by bus, stealing travel papers and identity cards to catch up with him. That's where she'd met Keely and learned all about Novo Mundum.

And here she was.

Carter suddenly noticed her staring at him. His face went white, then bright red. If she had been closer, Amber knew she would have been able to see the beads of sweat pop out but only on his temples, just like in those Japanese cartoons. She would have been able to smell his fear.

She had originally come here to catch him, to yell at him, and finally humiliate him—he thought he was so special being chosen for this elite community? Well, *look!* Amber Polnieki, thief and pregnant teenager, was here too. All she had to do was get up and quietly go over to sit next to him. Just *sitting* there, not saying anything, would probably give him a heart attack.

She looked down at her rounded belly. Amber had *hated* the fat little tummy at first, the vomiting, the pasty skin and puffy eyes. Now it was like she had gotten a second wind: her nails and hair were shiny and beautiful, and her face glowed.

And when you thought about it, she was here *because of* Carter. Because of the baby, because of his disappearance, she was in Novo Mundum, safe, secure, well fed, and surrounded by friends in a world that was rapidly going to shit outside. Here she was in paradise, and was she actually wasting energy thinking about pinging this boy, this *stupid* boy who'd led her here?

Forget it.

She turned away from Carter to look back at Dr. Slattery.

"We have little children growing up here," he was saying. "And soon we'll have more. These children are our future, and I won't let anything threaten or harm them."

And neither will I.

SIXTEEN

"SOUNDS LIKE SCIENCE FICTION," KEELY SAID, WALKING OUT with some of her fellow teachers. Though the day had been mild, the night was very firmly rooted in autumn: chill and dry, with sharp stars overhead. *Actually, everything about this place is science fiction,* Keely thought with a smile. The scene down the hill, on the main campus, was surreal.

Here and there electricity worked: the research lab was lit within, several fluorescent yellow windows indicating the scientists inside working hard on a vaccine or palliative for Strain 7. A few footlights lit up the prettier buildings: the library, the main liberal arts building, Alumni Hall, all faced in white marble and glowing richly like some fabled, ancient city. As soon as it got really dark, the lights would be turned off, and the entire campus would go dark behind blackout curtains in the windows to hide Novo Mundum from government satellites.

In, around, and between the other buildings more organic firelight flickered. Some people were socializing in the dorms by candlelight, and some people were still working outside on the lawns next to bonfires and torches. Sometimes someone would come by with a PalmPilot, its eerily steady blue glow making it look alien.

This was as close to a college campus as Keely was probably ever going to get—these days, anyway. The government was trying to set up smaller training facilities and universities—MacCauley was a fascist but not an idiot; America still needed scientists and doctors and teachers—but nothing like the Ivy or little Ivy she had hoped to attend.

Her mom, of course, had originally wanted her to stay close—Berkeley, maybe. But as much of a California girl as Keely was, she'd wanted to go to a small, old-fashioned East Coast sort of school. Williams or Wesleyan or something. *A campus pretty much like this,* she realized. A main square with the major lecture halls on it, as well as a library, and a cafeteria. Okay, so now the classrooms were sometimes used for drying vegetables and drying linens on rainy days, but they were classrooms nonetheless. In opposite directions on cobbled paths away from the square were the dorms—still used as dorms—the athletic fields, and the gym and tennis courts, not really used for anything. Beyond the main campus were the music and drama departments, where students had once been able to practice and exhort to their hearts' content.

And of course there was the main green before her, where students might have talked about philosophy and played guitar and ultimate Frisbee—now sparks flew from makeshift buildings where blacksmithing and metalworking occurred, where Mundians were relearning the basic crafts of human survival while mapping out a loftier future.

But everyone was happy with the work. Everyone smiled. Some wore the first generation of homespun clothes, rough, pale things, to save their jeans for special occasions. Others wore full suits to mock the previous system. It was a little silly, but Keely was relieved to be in a place where things could be silly again. Where there was rest, and discourse—and hope.

"Yeah, those tracking chip things sound really cool," said Bela, interrupting her thoughts. Her husband, whom she'd met and married at Novo Mundum, was in San Diego as N.M.'s main operative there. He was due back in a couple of months. *But it must seem like forever without any contact,* Keely thought.

"I don't know," one of the other teachers, who taught history, put in. "Don't you think it's a little . . . extreme?"

No one answered her; their cool looks were enough. Besides Bela's feelings, you just didn't disagree with Dr. Slattery—at least not aloud. All of these

people would have been eating protein bars and following MacCauley's orders in the half-dead cities that
were left on the coasts if it wasn't for Dr. Slattery and
his Novo Mundum.

Although the idea of having a chip implanted in her
arm intimidated her too, Keely knew she'd feel a lot
better about going on their adventure tomorrow if she
knew there was some way they could find and rescue
her, Gabe, and Michael if something happened. If they
didn't return when they were supposed to.

There was a time, not so long ago, when her mom
freaked out if Keely wasn't home when she said she
would be or wasn't exactly where they said they would
meet. As Bree and her father sickened and died, her
mom was terrified of losing Keely as well.

But Keely had lived.

And her mom had died inside.

And then she didn't care anymore where her daughter was, who she was with, or when she came home.
And didn't read the little messages Keely left her
explaining where she was and who she was with and
when she was coming home. And didn't thank her for
the meals Keely made and left her to eat after a long
day at the hospital.

Keely stopped, letting the rest of the group go on
without her. She knew her mom hadn't chosen to with-
draw and become the bitter non–mother figure she was.
She was unhappy because of the world she had been
forced into, work and death and no reward.

Here, on the other hand . . .

At Novo Mundum, Keely's mom could rest, sheltered from that world. She could do what she did best—work on immunology and research new vaccines, not set limbs and treat the sick and dying sixteen hours a day. She could return to the person she was before Strain 7. Maybe.

As she thought about it, Keely saw Jane, Dr. Slattery's "information specialist." She was hurrying somewhere with a notepad tucked under her arm and a perpetually frustrated look on her face. Keely jogged to catch up with her.

"Hey, can I talk to you for a second?" she asked politely.

"I have to deliver these notes to the research lab," the woman answered.

"Okay. Well, I was wondering if I could just talk to you about my mom—"

"You can't contact her," Jane snapped without so much as a breath. Keely had to bite back a response. Dr. Slattery was probably approached all the time by people who wanted loved ones to join them, but the other girl—what was she, twenty-five?—didn't need to be so rude about it.

"It's not just for me," Keely protested, hoping it wasn't a lie. "She's a research immunologist, just like Dr. Slattery. . . ."

"We know. We also know that Dr. Gilmore is doing research for the government. Even if we could make an exception for your mother, her current role makes that option completely impossible."

Research for the government? "No, they have her working down at Mount Sinai, in triage. . . ."

Jane allowed herself a quick, cold smile. "Not exactly."

Keely thought about how tired her mom was every day, how she just slept on the couch or stared blankly at the TV—which was usually off, since there wasn't much programming since the virus. It had looked like all the symptoms of physical exhaustion—but now that she thought about it, she couldn't actually remember any bloodstains or chemical smells or *any* clues that even the cleanest doctor might occasionally bring home.

"Well," Keely began awkwardly—*I'll think about all that later.* "Even more reason to get her away from MacCauley . . ."

"Look." Jane stopped, turned around, and faced Keely. She was only about five feet tall, but when she planted her short, muscled legs and glared up at her, Keely got the impression that this woman had faced down executives and presidents in her past. "You know they asked both of us to join? Me *and* my husband? But Tito didn't like the whole Novo Mundum philosophy. He's still stuck in the mind frame of *personal* growth and competition and dog-eat-dog and all that other pre-Seven businessman crap. So he didn't come. He's as good as dead. That sound cold, Keely? That's how Novo Mundum *survives.* Loyalty and secrecy."

"I didn't know she was working for the government," Keely mumbled, sort of in apology. She felt like she was in trouble. "Maybe I could talk with Dr. Slattery—"

"You talked with me. I said no. That's the end of it, Keely. My job is to make sure Dr. Slattery's time isn't wasted with things like this."

Keely's jaw actually dropped; she couldn't believe she was being talked to so rudely.

"She's better off thinking you're dead. At least *she* can move on," Jane said, turning on her heel.

Ouch. What was with that woman—why'd she have to be so harsh? Didn't she realize they were talking about Keely's *mother*? The only living close relative she had left?

Watching Jane march into the distance, Keely thought of all the hard choices people made when joining Novo Mundum. Even if they did it accidentally, like Michael, who was forced to leave his entire life behind. His father probably really *did* think he was dead.

"What was all that about?"

Gabe strolled up to her, chewing on a piece of . . . something, jerky probably. His entire lower face moved as he bit down, and Keely was suddenly reminded of Bugs Bunny. She tried not to laugh, and the tension of her previous conversation began to slip away slightly.

"Oh, I just was asking if I could talk to my mom," Keely said, sighing. "I can't," she added.

"Yeah, I have a family out there too—but, uh, we're better off that way. I thought you guys were arguing about something else, something interesting. It looks like her panties are in a serious twist."

"Definite power issues. She doesn't want anyone *near* Dr. Slattery."

"Yeah. Well, it's pretty well known that his 'information specialist' doesn't have a clue about anything. She's just a big ol' bag of wind and rules."

Keely bit her lip. "She's got incredible computer access, doesn't she?"

Gabe nodded. "She's an overglorified systems administrator. She and a couple of other guys switch off the actual upkeep of the system, and she oversees the e-mail and everything else. . . . Wait, what are you saying?" he suddenly asked, his thick black eyebrows drawing together.

"She just told me about her husband, who's still out there—I don't know, what if her whole being-a-bitch thing is just an act? I mean, if anyone could leak out information, she'd be in a pretty sweet spot to do it."

Gabe looked grim. "You and Michael and your conspiracy theories—but you might have a point. I never would have thought that. We should talk to him about it after the briefing tonight."

They began walking to their meeting at security and communications—what was once the math lab. One by one, the buildings began to blink out and disappear into the darkness as curfew was called and the electricity shut off.

"Hey, you know that stuff the elves eat on trips, like in *Lord of the Rings*?" Gabe asked, pulling out another stick of jerky.

"Lembas bread," Keely answered promptly, trying not to think of the last time she had actually seen a movie in an actual movie theater.

"Yeah. This shit ain't that."

SEVENTEEN

AT LEAST A THIRD OF NOVO MUNDUM—ANYONE WHO WASN'T actively engaged in work that morning—gathered at the river dock to see the three of them off. It was awe inspiring to look out at all of the faces. Michael had been there barely a month and already he was well known, respected, and liked. And he was doing something *important*— bringing back the equipment for the fences and the chips that would initiate one of the biggest changes ever at N.M., ushering in a whole new era of safety.

But in some ways, it was frightening looking at the community: there really were so few of them compared to the outside world.

I'll do everything I can to protect them, Michael vowed. *It begins here.*

Keely was hugging some of her students and some of the other teachers—both groups looked equally anxious. Only about half of the expeditions sent out beyond a hundred miles had returned successfully, all of the people intact.

The night before, Frank and Ellen had spent several hours going over the giant map of the Big Empty that covered an entire wall of the situation room. There was a neat spiral of blue pins, clustered close where Novo Mundum was and growing farther and farther apart away from it, where successful supply expeditions had mapped out a town and brought back all of its portable resources. Gray pins indicated areas they hadn't explored or had to turn back from. Random clusters of red were known base camps of the Slash—although since many of the gangs were nomadic, the information couldn't be relied on. Green pins, much more orderly, showed where MacCauley's army had field camps and what roads they most often used as supply lines. Black pins were for miscellaneous nastiness— anything from known violent survivalist groups to nuclear waste sites.

"Since you'll be going farther than any of our previous missions, we also need you to bring back additional information on the outlying areas," Ellen had said. "Colonel Slattery has a smaller map made up for you, with places marked where additional resources might be."

Each of them had a copy of the map—mimeographed, some ancient paper-copying process that made everything purple and blurry. On the other side was a page from some past student's paper on Wordsworth. Laser printed, of course.

Everyone who had traveled to Novo Mundum with Michael and Keely showed up, even Diego, who stood on one side of Irene. Jonah stood on the other. Michael saw Gabe and Keely exchange significant glances over that. Amber actually hugged Keely goodbye—it was weird how well the two girls, complete opposites in every way, got along. Even as roommates.

"I can't believe you can't drive," Amber sneered at Michael, but it was with a touch of playful lightheartedness he had never seen in her before.

"I'm the commander." He shrugged, smiling. "They're the go-to guys."

"*I'm* the commander, Private," Gabe corrected, throwing their duffel of supplies in the back of the jeep. "You're just a talky New York boy."

"That's right," Frank said, gruffly with just a little smile. "Remember that, you two. This boy here has had *real* military experience."

"Yes, sir." Keely saluted.

"There's an extra jug of gas in the back," Ellen said, "but you're still going to need to find more for the trip home. Also in there are three *empty* canisters—try to bring them back full. We're running low for the generators. There's a short and a longbow in the back, and hunting-tipped arrows, and *this.*" With great ceremony she handed a tiny Saturday night special over to Gabe. There was nothing more powerful than shotguns and handguns at N.M.; there were always discussions of stealing more powerful weapons from the army, but it hadn't seemed feasible yet. "You've got five bullets. Try not to lose it."

"Yes, ma'am," Gabe said, cocking it, feeling the heft of it, releasing the catch, and putting it in his belt.

"I think my mom had one of those," Keely whispered.

"L.A. girl. I'm surprised you didn't have three," Michael whispered back. As serious as this occasion was, there was something exciting about it, too.

"All right, this is it, folks," Frank said, stepping back. "Keely, Michael, Gabriel—good luck. Oh, and Michael." He lowered his voice and put a hand on his shoulder. "You make sure you return in one piece. My brother and I don't want to see our little girl grieving."

Michael's back straightened and his chest raised almost of their own accord; he couldn't help preening a little. Not only did Frank and Paul trust him as a leader, it sounded like they might actually approve of his and Liza's relationship.

As if on cue, Liza melted out of the crowd and hugged Michael—it was a little embarrassing; her eyes were large and wet. Ellen and Keely and Gabe carefully looked the other way. The solemnity of the moment was destroyed, but as her warm arms wrapped around his shoulders, Michael stopped caring.

"Come home safe," she whispered into his ear.

"Of course I will."

Of course he would. He was doing it for Novo Mundum and her. He *would* return, triumphant.

EIGHTEEN

THIS IS GREAT, KEELY REALIZED, HER HAIR FLYING AROUND HER ears.

She drove down a movie-perfect flat road that cut through prairie like a black marker on oak tag. They were getting some pretty good speed now; it was a decent highway that hadn't deteriorated much in the last two years. Some of the smaller ones they had been on—mostly when Gabe was driving that morning—were almost impassable; besides the usual potholes and disrepair, survivalists, including the Slash, and soldiers from MacCauley's army had purposefully dynamited parts of the road. Especially the bridges.

Kelly *loved* the jeep. She used to dream of owning a Porsche 911 Turbo S, but this completely changed her mind. Although it was great just to have a stick shift under her hand again, to be *driving.*

And yeah, she knew what they were doing was incredibly dangerous—but it was also incredibly exhilarating. They were on an *adventure,* Lewis-and-Clark style: mapping out unknown areas, eating dried fruit and pemmican and drinking bottled water, avoiding the natives, exploring a whole brave new world. Before the virus hit, there was no real exploring to do. Keely had read how like 100,000 people went through even *Timbuktu* every year. Every national park was mapped out; every back road could be found on a DeLorme map or satellite.

But now it was all new again. The whole Midwest had been evacuated by MacCauley's army, its population too ravaged by Strain 7 to support a sustainable infrastructure. Not exactly wilderness, not exactly populated, the Big Empty was an unknown no-man's zone. *Here there be tygres,* Keely thought, thinking of ancient maps and remembering the words printed on the back of hers.

The land they drove across was flat as a mirage. Grass grew up to the road and sometimes through it, fast weeds getting a foothold in cracks in the pavement. Two years of humanless presence had had little effect on the landscape, but where it was noticeable, it was disturbing. There was the obvious: evacuated, empty towns, rusted gas stations. A McDonald's whose golden arches were decorated with vultures. Gabe and Michael were particularly alert through these areas, stock upright with gun and bow. Once they thought they saw someone, a movement in the shadows that seemed too upright to be a coyote's, but it scuttled away and left them alone.

The subtler signs of emptiness were more upsetting: dozens of miles of perfectly straight and even telephone poles along the highway and then one down, hanging from the wires, leaning into the road. Hit by lightning, maybe. Unrepaired. Cornfields whose rushed harvest resulted in acres of brown stalks, leaning and finally falling to the ground in complete disorder. Nothing grew up to take their place; the genetically modified seed corn couldn't grow without the heavy help of humans.

Keely thought about the protein bars and coupons and rations everyone outside of Novo Mundum had to deal with. Where was the food coming from if not the Midwest, the breadbasket of America? She hadn't thought about it before. Were there enough farms on the coasts to support those who remained? Did the army take over the old agribusinesses?

As they crested a long, ramping hill—more like a roll in the landscape—they came on the most surreal image yet: fields and fields of sunflowers, hundreds of thousands of them, browning in the perfect autumn yellow sun. Like someone had reached down from the sky and drawn a line of blight across the landscape, desiccating and killing everything in its path.

Keely stopped the jeep, and neither Gabe nor Mike objected, also overcome with awe.

"I'll bet they were for sunflower oil or something," Michael said, lowering his bow.

"Wish I had a camera," Gabe said, leaping down out of the jeep. Keely didn't think it was a prizewinning shot. Up close the flowers were more like giant, faceless people with their heads cocked, listening to something she couldn't hear. "It's 1400 hours, people—seems like as good a place for lunch as any. What do you say?"

"Sure," Keely said, unable to tear her eyes from the giant flowers. She turned off the ignition.

Once the motor was dead, silence overtook them like it had been waiting in the shadows. From time to time the breeze in the stalks made little rustling noises, and once in a while a crow called, but that was it. For some reason it made Keely think of the beach at the end of the day, when almost everyone had gone home. No radios, no kids screaming, just the waves and the sky and natural sounds.

"We should bring back a bunch of these heads," Michael said, taking a slug of water from a canteen. "For their seeds—can't you make ethanol out of sunflower oil or something?"

It was a great idea and a perfectly pragmatic statement, but Michael's comment irked her for some reason. It was like he was completely unaffected by the world around him, focused only on progress, and ideas, and Novo Mundum.

Which was kind of a shame, because in the afternoon sunlight, his skin kind of glowed and his blond hair shone—the platonic ideal of the all-American boy.

Keely shook her head, clearing her head of the thought. It brought too many other things with it: sadness and pain and loss. Not worth it.

"You're thinking of biodiesel." *She* had participated in high-school science fairs too.

"Well, you can fry in it, this I know," Gabe drawled, opening their duffel bag of supplies. "I'm getting mighty sick of having my eggs fried dry—what the . . . ?" Something bright red and white fluttered in his hand, caught by the wind. It billowed out and floated gently to the ground.

A white-and-red-checkered tablecloth.

Keely laughed. "How perfect!"

"How frickin' weird," Gabe muttered, but looked for stones to weigh down the corners.

Their lunch was hard-boiled eggs, which Keely used to hate until the rationing began. Then she missed them, even when the insides were cooked too long and were bright green and smelled of sulfur. There were heels of whatever bread the scientists and cooks were working on lately, having a minimum of normal wheat and a limited range of yeasts. And apples—bright, shiny, and red. Keely saved hers for dessert, biting into it with relish.

"You look like a regular Eve sitting there like that," Gabe said, lying back with his head resting on his hands. He got up and leaned forward. "You wanna commit original sin with me, baby?"

It was so over the top that Keely cracked up. There was a sparkle—no, a *spark*—in his eyes that made the whole thing actually sexy. Gabe was just the sort of guy she was always a sucker for—dark, flirtatious, with a kind of playfulness she found extremely attractive.

Like Eric.

"We're on a mission here, people," Michael reminded them. He also lay on his back, hands behind his head, soaking up the sun. Relaxed for once. In his faded blue T-shirt he finally looked less like a wannabe businessman and more like Clark Kent—the one from *Smallville*. Especially when he smiled.

And then the clamp came down inside. *No.*

She was amazed at any reaction to boys these days, ever since Strain 7 had taken Eric. But two at once? And Michael wasn't even her type. Too normal and clean-cut. Type A. If she thought too much about it, though, the tearing began; something inside her ripped a little and reminded her of what getting too close could result in. She concentrated on finishing her apple, and looking at the sky, and pretending the rest of the world was okay.

"So. Michael," Gabe drawled, obviously about to start something. He was in the backseat, sprawled, a piece of grass in the side of his mouth. He had no problem letting Keely drive until dark; as a better shot, he was more useful as a wingman.

"Yes, Gabriel?" Michael asked, grinning. He was still laid-back, even hours after lunch. It was nice.

"You and Liza. Quite a touching good-bye."

"Yeah? She's nice," Michael said, still grinning, not looking back at him.

"'Nice'? My friend, you two were practically *vertical* doing the horizontal."

"We have *not* slept together," Michael protested but bit it off too quickly; the "yet" was left hanging.

"And poor Maggie is just a memory." Gabe sighed, taking off his cap and running a hand through his closely shorn black hair. "You're going to leave a string of broken hearts across the Big Empty. What was she like, anyway?"

"Pretty. Nice. Sexy. Smart when it suited her," Michael said, sighing a little.

"Vapid," Keely added. "Useless, whiny, dramatic, slutty when it suited her."

Gabe and Michael stared at her in shock.

"C'mon, Keely," Gabe said, "don't hold back, darlin'. Tell us what you *really* think."

Keely just grinned, concentrating on the road. *They didn't know I had teeth.*

"What do you think happened to her, anyway?" she wondered aloud in a completely different voice, as if she had never said the previous thing.

"With my luck, she's probably the mayor of St. Louis by now," Michael grumbled.

Keely threw back her head and laughed, inadvertently giving Gabe a face-full of her hair. He coughed and swept it out of his eyes. "Damn it, woman—we're on a mission. That's not a regulation cut."

Keely shook her head, pretending to fix it while letting more of it fly back. "Oops. I just—" She stopped. Something tickled her nose, very subtle and vague. An unnatural scent that stood out against the dirt and grass and dusty pavement. Something burning. Something oily. "Do you guys smell something . . . ?"

Michael sniffed the air. "No, I—"

"Fire." Gabe pointed, suddenly alert, no longer the

drawling hick he pretended to be. A thin, wavering line of smoggy brown danced up almost invisibly ahead and to the west.

"Should we go around?"

"Negative," Gabe said slowly. "It doesn't look like a cook fire. . . ." He reached under his shirt and pulled out a pair of tiny binoculars, the kind usually used by bird-watchers or operagoers. They looked ridiculous in his hands, but Novo Mundum didn't want to risk the potential loss of any better optical equipment. Keely kept driving since she hadn't been told otherwise.

The wind changed direction and suddenly the smell of burning rubber assaulted them, acrid and thick.

"I think it's a vehicle. I don't see anyone moving. . . . Keep driving," Gabe ordered.

Before there had been no real landmarks to help gauge their distance or speed; now they drew up to the wreck surprisingly quickly. It was off the side of the road in a ravine, barely visible from the road except for the smoke and shiny heat waves. They got out of the car, Gabe leading, gun at ready.

"Oh my G—" Keely turned her head quickly, closing her eyes. Even after everything she'd seen, all the death, this was by far the most horrific sight of her life.

NINETEEN

LETTUCE SEEDS WERE THE HARDEST. AMBER FROWNED, TRYING to concentrate, trying to get one seed at a time into their individual little holes. There couldn't be any waste, especially heading into winter, when all the greens they had were what they could raise.

"Ninety-eight," she whispered, "ninety-nine . . ."

Suddenly the irrigation system came on, harder than its usual "mist" setting, soaking her head and scattering the rest of the seeds from her hand onto the muddy table.

"Sorry!" a familiar voice called.

"Jonah . . ." She groaned as he came around the corner, a pipe wrench in one hand and a hose in the other, looking far less abashed than he should have. He squeezed the trigger once to empty the remaining water and managed to aim it at Amber's feet. "Cut it *out!*" she snapped. "I have to find like all these seeds now—it's not funny!"

"Look at you, so serious," Jonah said, shaking the rest of the hose and coiling it neatly. "What happened to the street girl who didn't care about *anything*—or anyone else but herself?"

"Yeah, well, that just shows how well you know me. *Zero.* You don't know *anything* about me." She pushed her fingers through the dirt angrily, trying to find the seeds by feeling them. "And by the looks of how you're *not* fixing the irrigation system, you obviously don't know anything about Novo Mundum, either."

"What are you talking about? I knew far more about it than you did when we first came here—*I* was chosen, remember? You were the urchin."

Amber's face burned. *They took me in. I'm just as worthy as he is*—more. Like, she had a baby. And *he* was a jerk.

"And if you ever stuck your head outside of your plants and the greenhouses, you might actually learn a thing or two," he continued pushing.

"Oh yeah, like what?" She couldn't even see the plants in front of her.

"Well, like the fact that Diego's leg is getting worse, even with the antibiotic ration they gave him."

"You only know that because you're sniffing around Irene," Amber shot back. "And that's something *everybody* knows."

Jonah glowered, his dark eyebrows coming together.

"Yeah? Do you even know about the spy, Little Miss Big Shot?"

"What are you talking about?" she asked, trying to sound bored. But she stopped pretending to work.

"Well, as Michael told, like, *everyone else* in our group, that guy Finch who disappeared as good as told him right before he left that someone *inside* Novo Mundum led the soldiers directly to the campus."

Amber fidgeted, shifting her growing-uncomfortable weight from one foot to the other. She had to pee again. Suddenly the greenhouse wasn't a haven; it was hot and uncomfortable and itchy. She wanted to scream at Jonah to *go away* but had to hear more.

"You're just a bunch of paranoid freaks," she said. "Who the hell would want to screw up this place? It's *perfect*. Nobody has any reason to."

"Someone working for the government would. Keely thinks it's Slattery's assistant Jane 'cause she used to be a sys admin at a big corporation and she's got the best access to the outside world through her computers. Also, she has a husband out there."

Amber didn't say anything; she barely knew Jane. She just thought of her as the tightly wound Filipino woman who ran stuff.

"Michael thinks it's Dr. MacTavish—apparently she's a bit of a troublemaker, and he caught her arguing with a guard, trying to get into the research facility." Jonah leaned over her. "So if you *actually* care about Novo Mundum, you'll keep an eye out. Like, for things besides your flowers."

As he trudged off, slipping the wrench into his belt, Amber was almost overcome with the urge to pick up a flowerpot and hurl it at his head. *Flowers.* What a dork. What she was doing was one of the most important jobs here, raising food for everyone. He was just a freak, acting all-important because he got to sit in on the home defenses meeting with Dr. Slattery and Frank.

"No better than a crappy plumber," she muttered, turning back to the planting bench.

But what if he was right?

She had finally found a place where she could deal, where she felt safe, where she could raise her baby safely and happily in an otherwise screwed-up world. Her life on the streets and with her waitress mom seemed like a dream since Amber had come here, a bad dream that was finally over.

And now someone was trying to ruin it.

TWENTY

"IT MUST HAVE HAPPENED RECENTLY," GABE SAID, HIS VOICE thick. Even the soldier wasn't unaffected by the scene. "Looks like birds haven't discovered them yet."

Michael had to swallow several times before he was sure he could keep from puking. Now was not the time to be weak. *These are the times that try men's souls,* he told himself over and over, closing his eyes and opening them again, forcing himself to refocus on the charred remains of the jeep and the five corpses in it. The skulls were black and jaws were open, swinging in the breeze, still covered in bits of dead flesh. One of them still had an eye in its socket, baking in the sun.

Gabe surveyed the area nearby, raising his gun as he checked behind the jeep, looking through the binoculars.

Keely continued to avert her eyes but kept close and alert. She could take care of herself.

Suddenly Michael felt a chill pass through him as a sick idea found its way into his brain. *Jeep. Five corpses.* It was crazy—there had to be plenty of jeeps carrying five soldiers in the area. No reason to believe it was that one.

Praying his imagination was just on overdrive, Michael staggered forward, holding his shirt over his nose as he came closer to the bodies. The smell of burnt human flesh was unlike anything he had ever experienced before, awaking ancient fear and disgust. Closing his eyes for a moment to steady himself, he reached into the dead soldier's shirt and pulled out his dog tags.

Hernandez. Alfonso P.

Fighting between relief and the horror of having to do it again, Michael went to the next body. And the next.

On the fourth he found it.

Finch. Edward L.

Michael fell back, turning his head to the side. These were the soldiers that Finch had "let" himself be found by to save Novo Mundum. He must have grabbed the wheel or something, killed all of them.

"Gabe," he said hoarsely, holding out the dog tags.

The living soldier came over and picked them up, the tags flashing deadly silver in the light. "Finch . . ." he said slowly. "Christ."

"I just thought he was going to, you know, have to go back," Michael said. Strangely, he didn't have any urge to cry. Vomit, yes. Kick something, yes. But not cry. "Like, be a soldier again for MacCauley or go live in one of the cities or something."

"That—that's your friend Finch?" Keely asked. She turned around, obviously forcing herself to look at the body of the man who had given his life to protect Novo Mundum.

"We should give him a proper burial, but we don't have the time," Gabe said.

"At least—to keep the coyotes off of him," Keely stammered. "Maybe a quick trench, move the car on top of it?"

Gabe shook his head. "It's not safe here. Look at the back—" He indicated the rear of the jeep with his rifle: the metal was blackened and dented and shredded.

"It exploded *in*ward," Keely realized.

Gabe nodded. "Rocket launcher. I didn't think there was anyone left around here with access to that kind of technology; MacCauley's men cleaned most of them out. *We* don't even have any. Whoever it is, we're probably not as much of a threat to them as the army—not worth wasting a rocket on. But they'll be watching us— and probably have other weapons."

Michael looked around. He couldn't see anything on any of the horizons around them, but the sniper could be a mile away, hidden behind anything.

"Keely, I'm going to need you to keep driving," Gabe ordered, pulling himself together. "If I say *now,* you start swerving—evasive maneuvers. But whatever you do, *do not stop.* Do you understand?"

Keely nodded.

Good girl, Michael thought. He had complete faith in her.

The three of them got back in the jeep, silent now and for the next five hours. *I won't let him die in vain,* Michael vowed. They would find the locator chips. They would bring them back with the equipment for the electrical fence. They would install trip wires and Michael would *personally see to it that everything that could be done would be done.*

Gabe sat on the back of the backseat, gun in one hand, Finch's dog tags in the other.

TWENTY-ONE

IRENE, JONAH, LIZA, AND DIEGO SAT AROUND A PICNIC TABLE at afternoon break, shelling beans. At harvesttime everyone took on extra work. It wasn't really so bad, Irene reflected, feeling the sun warm her skin. They chatted and laughed, and while it was noticeably cooler than the week before, it was still nicer outside than in. The main green was dotted with dozens of other groups doing similar tasks, some grinding corn by hand. Very biblical—but more via *The Ten Commandments* than what she'd had to learn for her bat mitzvah.

Even Amber had consented to join them. It was rare to get her out of her greenhouse these days, rarer still to have her do something group related that wasn't a top-down Novo Mundum requirement. And Jonah was kind of a loner too, now that she thought of it. He mainly stuck to the hidden, dark places underground, happily re-laying out pipes and electric things and boilers.

They're kind of alike in some ways, Irene thought, smiling. From the way the two *hadn't* been interacting, though, she would never dream of bringing it up.

"'The complete development and maturation of the human spirit as well as that of the mind is the ultimate goal in group, and therefore personal, evolution,'" Amber read aloud with some difficulty. They took turns reading aloud for entertainment, mainly from Dr. Slattery's book *The Human Potential,* in which he'd first developed the founding tenets of Novo Mundum. The original version was published long before Strain 7; these were old, often-thumbed paperbacks. "'Society is a human ecosystem all its own, and it's time people learned not only that what a person does has an effect on others, but that when it is carefully preplanned, it can have a cumulative positive effect on the system. . . .'"

Irene cast a quick glance over at Diego. He looked content, if pale. As with Jonah and herself, shelling the beans was no problem for his able, nimble fingers. She hoped being out in the sun would do him some good— the antibiotics Dr. MacTavish had given him would take a few days to work, but even so, he should have shown *some* improvement. The swelling around his wound had gone down some, but he was still far too weak.

"They should be halfway there by now," Liza said suddenly, interrupting. Amber frowned at her.

"I'm sure they're fine," Irene said soothingly. She

was pretty positive Dr. Slattery's daughter was only hanging out with her and her friends because they were as close to Michael as she could get with him gone. Which was fine—the girl obviously needed a lot of support and attention. But no one talked about the thing they all knew about—the suspected saboteur. No one was sure how much Michael had told his girlfriend.

"You want me to finish this or not?" Amber asked, shaking the book.

"Actually," Diego said slowly, "I wouldn't mind discussing it some."

"Fine with me," Amber said, putting it down. "It's a little highfalutin for a girl like me. I'm going to get some water. Anyone else want?" Even if they did, no one wanted the pregnant girl to carry more than she had to, so she shrugged and left when no one said anything.

"He seems to be saying that it is impossible for humans to live as individuals and achieve their potential," Diego said slowly. He fumbled with one of the beans.

"Absolutely," Jonah agreed. "Later on, in the chapter 'Group Dynamics,' he goes into greater detail."

"'Two's company, three's a team," Irene chimed in. She didn't care about the philosophy so much, but it definitely worked out well in practice in the medical wing. Having three people on staff at all times just made sense. *And my family makes a perfect team of three too.*

When their little group had first showed up at Novo Mundum, she'd been terrified that her dad and brother hadn't made it. They weren't there to welcome her, and she had to endure what seemed like hours of "processing": interviews and lectures and explaining about Diego and Amber and why they were there. Finally, when they were assigning roommates, Paul Slattery had looked at her with a smile and said, "But of course you'll live with your family."

Aaron and her dad were waiting outside; Irene had flung herself into her dad's arms like a little kid and wept in relief.

"We were worried about you," Aaron had said, punching her on the arm. "You took so long, we thought you weren't going to make it."

"I *knew* you would, Ree," her dad said, kissing her on the forehead. But there were tears in his eyes too. "Let's go home."

Home. It was an old fraternity house they shared with two other families—as familiar and lived in as anyone could want. There was a girl upstairs who intrigued Aaron because of the comic book collection she'd managed to bring. There was a small garden out back. There were good smells from the kitchen, and there was her dad, who looked content for the first time since Irene's mom died.

"Yeah, but weren't some of the greatest inventors . . ." Irene was pulled back into the present by Diego, who was still arguing with Jonah. He took a deep breath. "The greatest inventors," he said again. Suddenly beads of sweat popped out on his forehead. His face went even paler. "Alone . . ."

And then he collapsed backward onto the ground.

"Diego!" Irene cried, and ran around to him.

Everyone around them looked over and suddenly panicked, fleeing their work.

"Don't touch him," Liza warned primly, stepping back but not running. "They'll have to put you in decon, too."

"What are you talking about? This is just a fever from his *injury*," Irene said. "Somebody help me get him to the emergency room."

"Are you saying he could have 7?" Jonah asked Liza, surprisingly calmly.

"Or something like it. My dad's been studying various strains of it, hoping to develop a vaccine before something like this happened."

"It's not the virus," Irene snapped. "Now *come on,* people."

But Liza stepped aside, letting three hazard-suited men come around and approach Irene and Diego.

"Novo Mundum policy, Irene, you know that," one of the anonymous men said, taking her gently by the arm with his rubber-gloved hand. Like she was being summoned by a cartoon. "Forty-eight-hour quarantine."

"He's not sick!" Irene protested, but he pulled her away from Diego while the other two put him on a stretcher. "He's *not sick!*" she cried again, but even as she said it, she couldn't help feeling the fear spread within her, a tiny seed that had been nagging at her for a while now growing into something larger. Because why *hadn't* Diego's wound been healing better? What if something was really wrong with him?

TWENTY-TWO

"WE SHOULD PROBABLY PULL OVER SOON," GABE SAID, NODding at the road. "It's getting dark."

While they seemed to have avoided whoever had attacked the four soldiers and Finch, driving at night with headlights would have been suicidal. It would have been a beacon for every undesirable left in the Big Empty who might want a jeep, or the gas, or their supplies, or Keely.

She shivered at that and tried not think about it. Somehow it was almost more comforting to think of being randomly killed by a rocket launcher than being taken by the Slash.

Keely was exhausted from the drive and the fear that had replaced the earlier excitement. She tried to keep her eyes on the road, avoiding the larger potholes and obstacles. But every strange shadow, every metallic gleam in the prairie caused her to jump and worry until they were long past.

"There's a town or something up ahead," Michael said, looking through the binoculars. He was taking watch from the backseat now. Keely felt a little safer with Gabe and his gun next to her, but she felt none of the attraction she had that morning. She was too tired and he was all soldier now, not the usual playful, joking Gabe. "No lights—fire or anything."

"I think it's Springfield," Gabe said, looking at the map.

"Erewhon," Keely whispered.

"What?" Gabe looked over at her.

"Nothing." She shook her head. "It's 'nowhere' backward. I'm tired."

"You educated chicks . . ." He almost cracked a smile, but it vanished just as quickly. "We might as well hunt for supplies there too; it hasn't been touched yet. By us, at least."

"I think there's a Waffle House," Keely said, indicating a vaguely familiar sign that rose out of the night over them. Before Strain 7 it would have been lit, guiding cars in from the night like a lighthouse.

"Excellent. I've never been in one," Michael said.

"Are you *kidding* me?" Gabe asked, appalled. "Edjumicated girls and city boys. I'm frickin' *surrounded.*"

Keely was glad they seemed to be lightening up a little, but driving down smaller streets in the black, empty town didn't make her happy.

"We should explore the side streets and residential areas," Gabe continued, looking at the map. "See if the houses have been picked over yet. This place looks pretty untouched—could be a good resource for future expeditions." He indicated a smaller road for Keely to turn onto. It was still hard for her not to pause at intersections, waiting for a light—or at least another car.

The speed limit said thirty, but she was going fifteen, slowly cruising past little ranch houses closer to the highway, then more expensive ones farther in: two-floor family homes, hedges and gardens overgrown.

"The end of the American dream," Michael said, echoing her thoughts.

Nothing looked damaged—like the people had just picked up and left quietly. *I'll bet I'd find notepads, scribbled on, by the phones and stuff in the fridge, Keely* thought sadly.

"Let's go into that one," Gabe said, picking a house. It was a little more cheerful than the others, with an American flag hanging from its porch and a little less creepy garden. Keely pulled over and turned off the ignition. Once again silence embraced them, but here it was somehow closer and deader than on the prairie. Like the roses, Keely thought as she got out and stretched. They looked even more skeletal than they would normally in the fall. Not a single red rose hip on them to give the black-and-white town any color.

Michael jumped out of the car in one smooth motion behind Gabe. The ex-soldier was less jumpy than he had been at the jeep wreck, but his gun was still out.

She thought he was swaggering a little, maybe for her benefit. She wondered nervously if they were going to ask her to come with them or if she was going to be forced to stay with the car and break every horror movie rule: don't split up the party! Although she was so exhausted, it was hard to work up any real lasting dread.

No rose hips . . .

Suddenly something clicked her in mind. The American flag was *clean.* Well, mostly. But if it had been hanging out here for two years, it would have been tattered. And someone must have been deadheading the roses. . . .

"Gabe! Michael!" she shouted. "Someone's *here!*"

"It's okay," a voice said from behind. "It's just me."

Keely spun around. A boy, maybe twelve or thirteen at the most, stood there calmly with a paper bag of groceries in his arms, like he had just come back from a trip to the store for his mom. His clothes were neat and relatively new and he wore a *South Park* baseball cap.

Keely backed up, trying not to shriek, telling herself it wasn't a ghost.

"Who are you?" Gabe demanded, raising the gun.

"Jeremy. I *live* here," the boy said, with a faint smile. "You're welcome to come in, though. I was just going to make dinner. I'm sure Mom and Dad won't mind. We don't get a lot of new people around here."

Dozens of clichés flashed through Keely's mind: Put the gun down, Gabe, can't you see it's just a boy? and, We mean you no harm. . . .

"Even if you're not hungry, I'll bet you're thirsty. There's no water out there anymore." He jerked his chin toward the prairie. "Don't worry, I know a lot of bad stuff goes on out there, but you're safe in this neighborhood. *Really* safe. Trust me," he added, pushing past Gabe and Michael. He was short enough to walk under the gun and didn't look like he cared.

"Am I the only one creeped out by this?" Michael whispered as Jeremy took a key on a ribbon out from his shirt and carefully unlocked the door.

"Soldiers don't get creeped out," Gabe said firmly.

Keely and Michael looked at him.

"Okay, yeah, me too," he admitted. "But I think we should go in."

"It's okay—*Mom! Dad! Company!*" Jeremy shouted as he pushed open the door.

Keely went in first, Gabe following her closely with the gun. She figured that if they were a nice, normal, old-fashioned family, they would probably be put at ease by the presence of a girl in the group.

The house was dark inside and smelled a little stale, like an old classroom. Otherwise it was a fairly neat and normal suburban home.

"Sorry I can't offer you hot water to wash with—it'll take a few minutes to heat up," Jeremy said, putting the groceries down and flipping on a battery-powered lantern. "By the way, this is my dad," he said, indicating the couch.

Propped up on it was a rotten corpse, reading glasses still on, unopened can of beer in its skeletal hand.

TWENTY-THREE

THE QUARANTINE UNIT ON THE SECOND FLOOR WAS IN THE corner of the L of the old science hall and separated the general clinic and hospital area from Dr. Slattery's research labs. It was the only place in the building where there was still a way back and forth between the two areas. On the other floors the doors were locked and boarded over.

The unit itself was a lab that had been stripped of everything except for the stone-topped benches and a couple of chairs. The antechamber had been turned into a decontamination room where doctors could suit up and come in. Like Dr. MacTavish, who was in a full hazard suit, trying to look at Diego's leg as gently as she could with the thick-fingered rubber gloves.

Irene hugged herself, trying not to be freaked out by the scary scene. She would have to get used to a lot worse if she was going to be a doctor in the post-7 world, even on Novo Mundum. It wasn't just setting broken legs and delivering babies.

Liza sat in one of the few chairs, flipping through an ancient textbook on genetics, still pissed she had to endure the decon procedure. Jonah stood by Irene, close enough to offer emotional support but not creepy close.

Diego was lying on one of the stone lab benches, moaning and panting. Irene had taken off her sweater and folded it up to put under his head, but he didn't even seem to notice.

"All he did was collapse," Irene explained. "It really can't be the virus. He hasn't been off the grounds of Novo Mundum *once* in the weeks since we came here. He would have shown symptoms a long time ago if he had it. . . ."

Dr. MacTavish grunted, leaning over to stare in Diego's eyes, lifting one eyelid to see his pupil. Then she moved down to his leg.

"I think he's got a fever," Irene added hesitantly.

"His wound isn't healing properly at all," the doctor muttered. "I mean, the topical antibiotic seems to be helping the hole itself; there's the beginning of scar tissue—" She prodded it and Diego let out a heart-wrenching moan. Even Liza looked up, concerned.

"I don't get it. Shouldn't the antibiotics be working? I mean, he's a completely healthy, strong person otherwise—he lived by himself in the woods for years—"

"Honey, we ain't exactly got the best amoxicillin money can buy here," Dr. MacTavish said gruffly, but her eyes looked sympathetic. "He's on homegrown penicillin, and I had to *beg* for the latest batch from the cheeseheads in research and development."

"Maybe he needs more," Irene said hopefully.

Dr. MacTavish sighed. "Irene, I don't want to say this, but don't get your hopes up. There isn't a lot to go around and you're right—Diego *should* be healthy enough to take care of this on his own. In fact, he should have already." She frowned again. "Maybe he has an immune disorder?"

"I don't, uh, *think* so," Irene said as politely as she could. AIDS had sort of gone back burner since Strain 7.

"Damn it, I'm a dermatologist," the middle-aged woman swore. "I used to treat eczema and psoriasis and really bad acne. Foot fungus and skin cancer from too much tanning. Rich kids used to pay me to give them drugs to help clear up their faces—when they would have cleared up on their own in a few years." She closed her eyes and rubbed her masked forehead with her the back of her gloved hand.

"We know you're doing your best," Jonah said quietly.

"Obviously *not*," she spat, indicating Diego.

Nurse Chong came in through the door and double layers of vinyl with a clipboard and some bandages.

"Why didn't anyone notice his condition at his last checkup?" Dr. MacTavish snapped at the fat, serene woman.

"I don't know, Doctor, it wasn't my shift. He does

look terrible, though; I'll look into it."

"See that you do."

Irene thought she was being a little hard on the nurse; they were all overworked. Of course, why didn't Irene spot it herself before he collapsed? She felt a surge of guilt.

"Also, help me beg some more bread mold from Carver. This kid's really sick. Uh," she added quickly and apologetically to Irene, "I mean, right now."

"Can we get him out of quarantine at least?" Irene begged. "Now that you know it's the wound and not Seven causing the fever, he doesn't have to be in decon anymore, right? We can put him in a regular hospital bed."

"Sorry." Dr. MacTavish shook her head. "Out of my hands. It's one of Slattery's fundamental rules at Novo Mundum, and I can't say I disagree with it entirely. Personally, I think he's fine, but we're going to have to wait before releasing him or either of you two."

Liza sighed audibly, and Diego moaned again.

TWENTY-FOUR

"HOLY MOTHER OF—"

Michael was the last to see the carefully posed decaying body on the couch. He couldn't stop himself from staring; somehow the fact that the beer was Pabst was significant.

"Mom's upstairs, lying down," Jeremy said, carefully taking cans of tuna fish and bottles of cranberry juice and boxes of cookies out of the bag and putting them away. "You wanna stay for dinner? I can't cook as good as she can, especially on the little propane stoves. But we can have tuna and peas or something."

"Kid, this is screwed up," Gabe said, looking down at him.

"Oh, Jeremy," Keely said, eyes brimming with tears.

Michael was actually impressed by that. This was a

scene out of any—*really good*—grade-B horror flick and there she was, feeling all bad for the psycho kid who still lived with his dead parents and pretended they were alive.

"It's okay," Jeremy said shyly, looking up at Keely quickly before looking back down at the counter. "My gramma is going to come get me or send Uncle Todd. She'll come take care of me soon."

"When was that?" Keely asked as calmly as she could. "When did your grandma say she would come?"

Jeremy shrugged. "A couple of years ago, on the phone. But transportation's difficult these days."

Keely nodded, trying not to cry.

"Is *everyone* here dead?" Gabe asked directly.

Jeremy looked strange for a moment, like it was a new idea for him or something he hadn't thought about in a long time. "Everybody here is dead," he repeated, in almost exactly the same tone as Gabe. "But the decon trucks never came," he added brightly. "I guess they figured everyone was dead, so why bother? Springfield is so small, it gets skipped over a lot."

"Great. An entire *town* of corpses," Michael couldn't stop himself from saying.

"We are so out of here," Gabe muttered.

"Guys," Keely warned. "Of course we'll stay for dinner," she said, turning back to the boy. "We'd be honored."

"We *would* be, but we're not, thanks anyway," Gabe said, finally putting his gun away. It wouldn't do much against the dead.

"Yeah, sorry," Michael added.

Keely turned to them with a look that would have

frozen lava. She had lost a sister about the same age, Michael knew—*Bree*. Somehow the miniature Norman Bates before them had awoken maternal instincts in her, even in this house of the decomposing.

All joking aside, Michael really wasn't sure he could last another five minutes there, much less stay for dinner. He hadn't been able to stop thinking of Finch for the last few hours and the dead soldiers with him. The corpse on the couch just slammed it home.

There was a long moment of silence between the three.

"Uh? Am I setting for one or four tonight?" Jeremy prodded, holding up a bunch of forks.

"Four." Gabe gave in first, groaning.

"And we might as well spend the night here too," Keely added slowly, making sure the other two fully understood.

"Not *here*," Michael protested. "And we leave first thing in the morning. *First. Thing.*"

"Yeah, what he said," Gabe said, jerking his thumb at Michael.

"Great!" Jeremy said, smiling.

Actually, dinner wasn't so bad. The kid managed to make a sort of a tuna-pasta-and-peas thing with water he boiled on the little camping stove he had brought home. Full and empty mini bottles of propane were lined up neatly on the floor near the door.

He had set the table carefully, with paper napkins, and thoughtfully sat them so only he was looking at the corpse.

"It must be awful lonely living here now," Keely ventured.

"Nah," Jeremy said, stuffing his mouth like a normal, growing boy. "It's kind of boring because no one *new* comes here, but I don't think it's really safe out there." He indicated the rest of the world, or the Big Empty, with his fork.

"You got *that* right, kid," Gabe said grimly.

Michael took advantage of the pepper; it was strictly rationed at Novo Mundum, once again classified as an "exotic spice," as it had been hundreds of years ago. In fact, even compared to his life in New York after Strain 7, the food at Novo Mundum was kind of bland. They should bring a crateload of spices back with them. *That* would give them a hero's welcome even more than the locator disks, he thought, smirking.

"You could come *with* us," Keely suggested casually, as if she hadn't been thinking about it ever since they came through the door. Michael almost choked. He looked at Gabe, who was also giving her a horrified look back. "We're from a place that's safe and free. . . ."

"Yeah, I thought you might be from one of those communes or something," Jeremy said wisely. Then he frowned and looked scared—for just a moment. "I don't think Mom and Dad would like it if I went with anyone except for Grandma."

"Well, think about it," Keely urged. "Talk to, uh, your parents about it. We have a lot of other kids your age, *new* ones, you might like to meet."

"We should begin looking for a place to bunk tonight,"

Gabe said, looking at his watch. Michael breathed a sigh of relief as Keely's attempts were cut off. "We have to get going by dawn."

Finding a place they felt like they could stay was like a sick version of *Goldilocks:* each house had too many corpses, or dead cats and dogs, or other creepy things. The one they found that was the closest to "just right" seemed to be pretty empty, though they all decided not to check the basement.

"I, uh, don't mind sharing a room," Keely said nervously when they offered her the master bedroom; Michael and Gabe planned to sleep in the kids' room, which had a bunk bed. The smell of death was almost unnoticeable among the matching bureaus and bed, dust ruffles, and fancy silk comforter. But it was still *there,* underneath everything else, like a sour note in a sound track. And no one had slept by themselves since coming to Novo Mundum—there wasn't really room.

"I'll share the bed with you, if that'll make it better," Gabe said, leering a little.

"I'm not staying in that other room alone," Michael said quickly. "I'm chicken. I admit it."

"Let's *all* stay in the other room," Keely decided, leaning over and gathering up as much bedding as she could. "I'll even take the floor."

"Negative," Gabe said, sighing. "*I'll* take the floor, you soft-tushed civilians."

"I'll take the floor. I'm the second-biggest chicken

here—it's only fair," Michael decided, taking the quilt from Keely.

They each took turns in the bathroom with a candle. Michael enjoyed using as much toothpaste as he wanted, carefully cleaning all of his teeth with an extra brush he found in the cabinet. It wasn't like his old Sonicare, but it was nice at least to feel minty fresh again. There was even some mouthwash. Toothpaste came and went at Novo Mundum; often they used some homemade gunk that the gardeners kept promising they'd have enough mint to add to someday. He felt a little guilty that he was even using some of the old-fashioned, commercial stuff.

The floor wasn't so bad once he'd laid out a lot of pillows and folded the bedding over. It was like a really weird old-fashioned sleepover—Gabe was already snoring; Michael was pretty sure the soldier could sleep on a bed of nails. He listened to Keely toss and turn some before finally sighing and settling down. It was comforting somehow. It was strange and lonely to be out here by themselves after the friendly, slightly overpopulated dorms at Novo Mundum.

But soon he was asleep too.

TWENTY-FIVE

MICHAEL SAT UP, HEARING A NOISE.

He checked his watch; the eerie blue glow said that it was 3:17 a.m. Gabe was still snoring, and by the fading light of the candle stub he could see Keely's shoulders slowly moving up and down with sleep. He listened to the darkness, cocking his head, straining to hear over his own breath and heartbeat, which were extremely loud in his ears.

There it was again.

A scrape downstairs, the quietest thump of a shoe. Was it Jeremy, checking up on them? Or something far worse? Maybe the house wasn't entirely empty of its occupants after all. Maybe there were other freaks like Jeremy still here.

Michael knew he should wake Gabe and Keely, but

somehow it didn't seem right—especially after calling himself a chicken earlier. He could check this out by himself and keep them *both* safe and undisturbed. Quietly he rose, pushing the covers off him, and crept out of the room. Fortunately he was wearing his favorite flannel pajamas, so at least he wasn't naked. He stepped quietly barefoot down the stairs.

"Who's there?" he tried to say aloud, but nothing came out.

A figure stood in the shadows, a little too still, a little too stiff.

"Who's there?" Michael said again, this time managing a whisper. His heart was beating out of control now.

The figure lumbered forward into a patch of moonlight, so he could fully see his face.

"Finch!" Michael realized, overcome with joy. "You're not dead! It was a mistake!"

"You didn't come back for me," the soldier said. His eyes were blank and dead, and he held up his dog tags. "I *died* for you and you wouldn't even come back for me."

Michael froze. Of course Finch was dead. He knew that; he'd seen the body. So this was—

"*You're* the traitor at Novo Mundum!" Finch hissed. When he opened his jaw, Michael could see his teeth blacken and the flesh begin to shrivel, like he was burning from within. *"You let me die!"*

"No!" Michael protested, the tears beginning to run down his face.

But Finch lunged for him, his blackened fingers clawing for his throat.

Michael grabbed the balustrade and threw himself over the side of the stairway, landing painfully on the carpet. When he looked up, there was another Finch, sitting on the couch with a beer in his hand, just like Jeremy's father. It looked at him and laughed.

"No," Michael whispered desperately. "I didn't kill you. I want to *save* people; I want to stop this from ever happening again!"

"Too late for me, isn't it?" The figure leaned from the couch and fell forward at him.

Michael got up and ran. He fumbled at the front door; the doorknob stuck. He looked over his shoulder: there were three Finch corpses behind him now, only a few feet away.

Michael screamed and finally smashed the door open with all his strength. He ran into the street so hard that he tripped over himself when he stopped to look back at the house.

It didn't really matter, though.

There were dozens of corpses coming at him now, from up and down the street and out of all of the houses.

"Your fault," they wheezed, eyes burning red as they melted in their sockets. *"It's your fault!"*

Michael screamed.

TWENTY-SIX

JONAH AND IRENE BLINKED, TRYING TO GET THE STINGING decontamination fluids out of their eyes.

"You're only going to make it worse," Liza said, bravely trying to keep her own eyes open while tears ran down her cheeks.

After nurses had taken Diego away to keep a better eye on his condition, the three remaining had been led to a shower area, where they were sprayed with something *nasty* smelling. Irene tried not to show any fear for Jonah's sake, but anything that smelled that strong *and* killed all sorts of diseases on contact probably wasn't that good for their eyes, noses, or other sensitive, mucousoidal parts of their body.

Now they were in a secondary quarantine unit, left

with nothing to do but be bored . . . and worry about Diego.

"Well, this sucks," Jonah said, taking out the penknife he always carried with him and flipping the chain back and forth. "On the bright side, we're probably safer now than anyone else on the planet. No one would *dare* come near us."

"We don't have anything," Irene said wearily, with a faint smile. She sat down on a chair not too far from the soldier.

"Yeah, haven't you been listening?" Liza snapped. Her quick mood turnarounds reminded Irene of Amber when they first met her. Even though this girl was her own age, Irene had to remind herself that Liza had grown up in this secluded little paradise even before Strain 7. She was *very* young for her age. "Diego fainted because he's all sick, and we just had the misfortune to be nearby."

"Yeah, bummer about that," Jonah said, a growl in his voice. Irene patted his knee and shook her head so Liza couldn't see—*drop it.*

A door opened and someone in a haz-mat suit unzipped the inner flaps. When the slightly shaded visor turned in their direction, the visitor revealed himself to be Dr. Slattery.

"Diego's condition is looking pretty serious from what Nurse Chong told me," he began, "but probably nothing infectious that got to you guys."

He smiled at his daughter and tousled her hair with his green, heavy-gloved hand. With the single flickering fluorescent light behind him and reflections on his visor masking his face, Irene suddenly found the whole thing creepy. At least Dr. Slattery got to visit his daughter— what about *Irene's* dad and Aaron? They were probably worried sick about her.

"As some of you already know," Dr. Slattery said, smiling at Liza, "you have to stay on this floor, in this unit, for forty-eight hours. After that we can be positive nothing's wrong with you and you can go. And stay *out* of the research labs. Just because there's no guards posted there today doesn't mean it's safe. Okay?"

"Yeah, yeah," Liza said, but smiling, "we know."

"All right. Jonah?"

Jonah leapt up and all but saluted. Dr. Slattery smiled and put a plastic-armored arm around his shoulders. "I don't want to sound old-fashioned, but you take care of your two Novo Mundum sisters in here, okay? Entertain them, maybe. Can you sing?"

Jonah tried to keep from smiling. "No, sir. No, Dr. Slattery," he corrected quickly.

"Ah, well, I guess your talents had to end somewhere," the older man said, sighing theatrically. "Well, do what you can. I'll be back later."

After the doctor turned and left, Irene thought about how if it had been *her* dad visiting her, he would have tried to blow her a kiss through the mask or something silly like that. Dr. Slattery probably just had too many other worries running Novo Mundum and all.

"I want my mommy," Irene said sadly, with a smile. "Times like this, I really miss her."

"Mine died ten years ago, of breast cancer," Liza said, looking through the rest of the books that were left there to entertain them.

"Oh." Irene was taken aback—there was almost no emotion about it from the other girl, like she had cut off that part of her life entirely. "I'm sorry."

"At least she wasn't taken by Seven, like everyone else out there."

"I sure don't miss my mom," Jonah cut in, trying to lighten things. "*Or* the way she tanned my hide."

"Ugh, this is totally boring," Liza huffed, throwing the books aside. "I'm out of here." She unzipped the inner flap and reached for one of the haz-mat suits hanging there.

"Dr. Slattery said we were supposed to stay here . . ." Irene protested, rising to stop her.

"I *grew up* here. I know my dad's labs like the back of my hand," the other girl said, fumbling to close a catch with her gloved hands. Then she pulled over the head covering, tightened the neck, and was gone.

TWENTY-SEVEN

"MICHAEL! WAKE UP! MICHAEL!"

"Come on, buddy, snap out of it."

Sweating and shaking, Michael finally opened his eyes. He didn't seem to know where he was—sitting up in the middle of the floor, bedsheets twisted around him. Keely kept squeezing his hand, reassuring him that everything was all right. At least he had stopped screaming.

"I'm not wearing pajamas . . ." Michael said slowly, looking down at his naked torso. "It was a *nightmare*. . . ." He looked *terrible,* Keely thought, which was a rare thing to say about him. His face was pale and his eyes were sunken and red. His usual peach-healthy skin was clammy. "Finch . . ."

Keely felt a strong mixture of sadness and compassion for the second time that day. When she looked up at Gabe, he was trying to be the steely-eyed strong one, but there was sympathy in his eyes. "You dreamed about him?"

"He was everywhere. Dead—and rotting," Michael recalled, still breathing heavily. "And accusing me. Saying I didn't go back for him. That I *killed* him. That *I* was the one destroying Novo Mundum."

"Now, you know that isn't true," Gabe said, smacking him on the back. "It's just your subconscious or whatever."

"You're trying to *save* all of us at Novo Mundum," Keely said soothingly. She had the urge to stroke his damp hair, but something still held her back. "That's why we're out here."

"I know. I know." Michael leaned his head on her shoulder and closed his eyes. "It was just . . . I was so glad to see him at first. I thought he was alive or something."

"I had a dream like that too," Gabe admitted. "We were playing cards."

"Yeah, but you didn't scare the bejesus out of us by waking up screaming," Keely said, grinning down at Michael.

"That's 'cause I'm not a big ol' sissy boy," Gabe said, also smiling.

"Maybe I'll take you up on that offer after all, Gabe," Keely said, trying to think of a way they could all sleep better without embarrassing anyone. "Let's pull down those mattresses and camp out on the floor here. It'll be fun—and it will make *me* feel better. This place really creeps me out." She wasn't lying about that last part. It wasn't so easy getting back to sleep having been woken in a town of the dead by bloodcurdling screams in pitch darkness—even if you *weren't* the one with nightmares.

Michael looked grateful and even Gabe didn't object, immediately leaping up and wrestling with the mattresses, muttering something about an orgy of civilians.

And while she would have preferred one of the sides, Keely found herself lying in between the two guys . . .

Which actually wasn't that bad.

TWENTY-EIGHT

"WELL." IRENE SIGHED. "IT'S JUST THE TWO OF US NOW."

"Fine with me. You'd never guess that little *thing* was related to Dr. Slattery," Jonah said, rolling his eyes. He tried to hold with one of the basic tenets of Novo Mundum—love your fellow Mundian—but it was hard with people like Liza. And shouldn't the daughter of Dr. Slattery set an example for the rest of them? Jonah almost felt like *he* had a more appropriate relationship with the man. When he was growing up, he just wished that he had a dad who didn't beat him. Paul Slattery was everything he never dreamed of—but always unconsciously wished for—in a father.

Things would have been so different. . . .

"She's probably had very little love and attention

these last few years," Irene said, interrupting his train of thought.

Jonah never ceased to be amazed by her empathy—she would have a great bedside manner someday when she was a full doctor. But Irene was also obviously getting a little tired of making these excuses. The way Liza had talked about Diego before, it had looked like Irene was ready to sock the other girl.

"Yeah, well, join the club," he said, not going into detail. He didn't want her to pity him.

"Or, as I was going to say, she's just a little biyatch." Irene gave him a crooked smile. Jonah grinned back—it was nice to see even would-be Dr. Perfect had a limit. It was kind of sexy, too, seeing her nasty side.

"I wonder if there's a textbook or something around here I can read," Irene continued, squinting at various stacks of reading materials around the room.

"I'm sure there is. And . . . I'm sure someone told your dad and your brother that you're okay," he added gently. "The one thing Novo Mundum *really* excels at is speed of communication. Especially gossip."

"Thanks, Jonah," she said warmly, her dark eyes soft and sincere.

He thought about what his parents would say, knowing how he felt about a girl like this. Strain 7 hadn't seemed to break down any of their prejudices with a general love for who remained. Jonah shook his head, trying to forget the times his dad had used certain words to describe the people he blamed for ruining America. *The world really is better off with him dead,* he thought bitterly. Dr. Slattery was right—they had to change the future of humanity. Make it all right this time.

"I wonder where it would be," Irene said, suddenly looking away after he held her look for too long.

"What?"

"A medical textbook," she said patiently.

"Oh, I don't know. I'll help you look."

"In a little while, I guess. When we get bored."

"I don't think I could *ever* get bored talking to you." There. He'd said it. Shyly, but he'd said it. Jonah was pretty sure he was blushing and was glad it didn't show. But this was the only chance he had, without her worrying over Diego or having someone else around. There was *always* someone else around.

"Oh, Jonah, that's really sweet," she said with a compassion that nearly killed him. Then she reached over and hugged him, putting her head on his shoulder.

Even though he knew it was just a "pity" hug, Jonah almost died. Irene managed to smell of honeysuckles and comfort in a community where soap was a luxury. Her cheeks were soft and velvety—he would have given anything to be able to kiss them. She had kept her hair shorter since being at Novo Mundum, and he ran his fingers through it while patting her head.

But he gently let her go, *first,* so he wouldn't appear like a total loser. And rather than wishing harm on Diego, Jonah prayed for a quick and speedy recovery for him. Because how could he compete with a sick guy for the attention of a doctor?

TWENTY-NINE

WHEN KEELY FINALLY OPENED HER EYES THE NEXT MORNING, she realized she was holding Michael's shoulder. Gabe was pressed into her back, snoring. Their physical closeness was unnerving for a number of reasons—not the least of which was the fact that there was something indescribably sexy about the two guys' complete vulnerability. Even Gabe's face had softened as much as it could.

Some of the attraction died, however, when Keely sat up and got a full dose of Michael and Gabe's combined morning breath.

"Uh, guys?" she ventured.

Gabe spasmed awake and rolled up and off the mattress in one smooth motion when he realized where he was. "Oh, uh, morning, Keely," he mumbled, shame-faced. "Michael, get up!" He balled up a sock and threw it at him.

"Huh? What? Oh . . ." He looked around, confused. "Oh my God, Finch . . . last night . . ."

"I'm, uh, gonna use the bathroom," Keely said, excusing herself. The vibe was too weird. She would deal with it better after she used some of the cleansers and moisturizers she'd seen the night before in the medicine cabinet.

Breakfast was also awkward, for different reasons. They ate back at Jeremy's, who did a fairly decent job of making grits and powdered eggs. Michael and Gabe made a big deal of *not* looking behind them at the dead guy on the couch and shot Keely dirty looks whenever she tried pressing Jeremy to come with them again. But the boy kept politely refusing, saying he had to stay and wait for his grandma. When they finally drove off, he stood in the street, waving good-bye to them calmly like they weren't the first harmless, living people he had seen in the last two years.

Keely kept silent for several hours before she couldn't stop herself from bringing it up again.

"You know, I bet he would have come if you guys had backed me up."

"Would you let it drop, Keely?" Michael said, exasperated but amused. "We appreciate your whole maternal instinct thing, but that is one. Screwed-up. Kid. And he's done just *fine* for the last two years. I'm sure he'll continue to do . . .*fine.*"

"Yeah, Keels, taking him along would only have interrupted the mission," Gabe said from the backseat. Although, Keely noted, he was chewing gum from the pack Jeremy had given him before they left. "We're out here for Novo Mundum. To get the disks and the fence equipment so we can go back and *protect* ourselves and everyone. That's our job." He didn't say, *Remember Finch,* but checking in the rearview mirror, Keely saw the bleak and determined look on his face.

"Well, can we stop by again on the way back, when we're done?" she pressed.

"Negative. But when we get home, we'll tell Dr. Slattery about it and he'll decide what to do, okay?"

"He won't fit in there, Keely, if that's what you're thinking."

Keely turned to look at Michael—she had a feeling she wasn't going to like where he was going with this line of argument.

"Jeremy is *broken.* Tragic, yes—one of the millions of victims of Strain 7 who didn't die of it. But he is *completely* wack. He's not even *trying* to overcome his own insanity. No desire to do anything but exist in his own crazy little world—and Novo Mundum isn't about that. He's just not the sort of person the future needs—and definitely not a person Dr. Slattery would ask to join."

"You weren't asked either," Keely shot back.

"Yeah, but he's a freaking model citizen," Gabe said from the backseat. "He *should* have been tapped."

On the one hand, Keely could sort of see wanting to start the new world—Novo Mundum—with a community of young, enthusiastic, and intelligent people who got along great with each other, like superintelligent beavers or better-dressed Mennonites. But completely dispensing with the rest of the human race? Just because they weren't perfect or didn't agree with the Novo Mundum philosophy?

"It's like college, Keely," Michael said reasonably. "You wouldn't have expected someplace like Harvard to just take in anyone, right?"

"Hey, welcome to St. Louis," Gabe read as they passed the sign. "Where's this warehouse we're supposed to be looking for?"

Michael bent over the map, studying it. "Actually, the turnoff's not too far."

Gabe decided they should park the jeep, hide it somewhere, and continue on by foot; while a lot of the smaller towns they had been through were completely deserted, it was far more likely a major urban center like St. Louis would attract more survivalists, looters, and hangers-on. And the jeep, while great to drive, wasn't exactly silent.

They found a mall and parked in its garage, a place that might have been home to homeless people in the past. In the Big Empty you could choose from five-bedroom houses and penthouse apartments if you wanted. From the mall it was just a half mile past an old technology park—Keely wasn't sure whether to laugh or cry when she saw that one of the companies in it was the one that published the SAT-prep course she had just begun when Seven hit.

"Okay, we just make the next left, and it should be

two blocks down," Michael said as they walked around the corner of a fat and flat industrial building.

"'Blocks'?" Keely said. "What are you talking about, New Yorker?"

And then they looked up.

Right around the corner, just as surprised as the three of them were, five MacCauley soldiers stood in their gray-and-green khakis and gold patches, carrying semiautomatics. Which were rapidly aimed at them.

"RUN!" Gabe yelled, turning and pushing the two of them. Keely was confused for a moment—wasn't Gabriel a soldier too? Then she remembered the little tiny gun he had. Not really useful.

They booked back the way they came—Gabe grabbed Keely's hand and pulled her along. Any hope that they might not have been followed was dispelled by the heavy thud of the soldiers' boots against the pavement behind them. Someone fired a round; Keely gasped and doubled her pace.

Michael suddenly ducked sideways into a narrow alley between two buildings, disappearing. Gabe and Keely followed; he pushed her in front of him with one arm. At the other end of the alley was a big blue Dumpster—after running around it, Michael and Gabe threw their shoulders against it and knocked it over, blocking the alley with garbage. The footsteps paused and swearing began, but even as the three of them started to run again, Keely was pretty sure they weren't farther than a bullet could reach.

Gabe pointed across the road at a line of dead,

parked cars. They waited until he mouthed, *Go!* and tore across the open space, jumping and dancing to slip between the close fenders. At the top of a concrete flight of steps Keely was just wondering wildly how they expected to get inside the building they were now at in front of when Gabe pulled her along the cement "porch" and stopped, vaulting over the edge. It looked too far to the ground to her panicked eyes, but suddenly strong hands were around her waist; Michael lifted her, and she put her hands down on the concrete rail, pushed, and Gabe caught her as she fell. Michael dropped down beside her and they ran down another set of stairs that led to a janitorial area with several large recycling and garbage cans.

Gabe grabbed Michael's arm and pulled them both behind the cans.

They'll find us! Keely mouthed. This was just like her worst nightmares as a kid, where she was hiding from monsters someplace dumb and she *knew* they were going to find her; it was just a matter of time.

Can you outrun a marine? Gabe mouthed back.

Keely ducked her head down and tried not to breathe.

THIRTY

IRENE WOKE UP EARLY EVEN THOUGH SHE TRIED TO FORCE herself to go back to sleep, to use up more time unconsciously, to make the time left in quarantine seem shorter. *Twenty-nine hours to go.* She sighed. She could just barely see Jonah asleep on the cot in the connecting room. He breathed silently, his freckle-colored lips parted a little. Definitely cute, but sometimes he was a little much to deal with.

Liza had never returned that night; for one uncharitable moment Irene had imagined her curled up asleep in a dangerous-chemicals hood, like a puppy behind glass. That gave her an idea, though: if anyone caught her walking around places she wasn't supposed to be in a haz-mat suit, she could just say she was following

Liza's example. And that meant she could go find Diego.

As silently as she could, Irene pulled back the plastic from the door entrance on the "girls'" side and took a suit, buckling it up the way she had seen the other girl do it the night before. She paused for just a moment, wondering what kind of trouble she could end up in if she were caught. Did people get expelled from Novo Mundum?

I was just following Liza's example, she reminded herself. *I was just seeing if Diego was all right.*

Irene chanted this as she turned the knob as softly as she could, slipping out, just touching the door closed behind her. Bravery had never been her thing, except at the sight of blood. Maybe if she cried, no one would yell at her.

The hallway was ghostly silent at that hour—even the hardest workers at Novo Mundum didn't do science at five-thirty in the morning. Everything was bathed in a pleasing if slightly spooky gray half-light that made Irene think of wet spring evenings on the lawn at home. Some of the rooms were empty or used to store supplies, boxes of textbooks and beakers piled up on benches where freshman chem was once taught.

In one of them, farther down toward the end, however, research was evidently going on. There were neat rows of sealed petri dishes in glass cases, some empty of specimens, some with cloudy agar and ugly stains in the middle. Special microscopes that could be used with haz-mat visors were set up here and there, though there were no slides left in them. Irene picked up a notebook that lay nearby and started to read it; there were notes about the behavior of Strain 7, about a vaccine, and something called The October Project.

But before she got to anything really interesting—or that she could understand—Irene heard footsteps down the hallway, as tentative and tiptoeing as her own had been. Panicked, she flattened herself against the wall.

Dr. MacTavish was slinking down the hall and not in a haz-mat suit: just gloves and goggles and a surgical mask. She was looking around nervously, obviously afraid of being caught. For just a moment Irene was smug: *she* did a better job of snooping than the doctor.

Then she remembered what Diego had told her about the suspected saboteur or spy in Novo Mundum. Michael wanted her to keep an eye on the doctor, who was a little too outspoken against Dr. Slattery and who had tried to talk her way into this facility just a couple of days ago. Irene felt a twinge of guilt; she hadn't done such a good job of shadowing MacTavish because she kind of liked the gruff, older woman, who had taken her on as a sort of apprentice. She didn't at all seem like the type of person who had secrets—but now it was obvious she was up to something.

Irene wasn't sure she could walk without the haz-mat suit creaking or making a noise, so immediately following the doctor was out of the question. She just had to wait.

A few minutes later she heard rustling and the sound of boxes being moved around in the room next door. Trying to use those noises as a mask, Irene moved slowly but steadily into the lab across from the one she was currently in, one that gave a pretty good view into the room where Dr. MacTavish was moving things around. The older woman was looking for something a little desperately, opening cabinets and the giant cooler. She must have found it; Irene could hear a sigh of relief as the doctor stood up straight, a flat cardboard box in her hands.

Irene just barely pushed herself back against the wall in time as MacTavish rushed out, tiny brown vials tinkling against each other in the box.

She was stealing chemicals from Dr. Slattery's special research lab.

THIRTY-ONE

MICHAEL'S LEGS HAD CRAMPED, THEN FROZEN IN POSITION, then cramped again as the three of them sat hiding from the soldiers. The pain in his knees was almost unbearable—like choosing a bad position in hide-and-seek and being stuck with it, but with far graver consequences.

Eventually Gabe quietly moved from his position and signaled that the two of them should remain. For the ten minutes he was gone, Michael almost couldn't breathe, waiting for a gunshot.

"All clear." Gabe spoke in a surprisingly normal-volume voice as he came down the basement stairs, one hand on the balustrade, one hand holding the gun.

"They must have given up," Keely said, obviously as

surprised as he was that their minimal hiding place had actually worked. "Thank God."

"I wouldn't be too sure about that last part," Gabe said grimly. "They gave up *way* too quickly and easily if they really wanted to find us. Also, that round they shot before was over our heads."

"What are you saying?" Michael ran through possibilities quickly, but he knew his mind didn't work along the same lines as a trained soldier's.

"I'm saying that in our civvies"—he pulled at the neck of his faded Old Navy tee—"we look like three dumb kids who decided to stay behind, and they have bigger fish to fry."

"Slash?" Keely asked. She tried to sound businesslike, but the fear in her voice was unmistakable.

"Or something. Come on—we'll find someplace to hide until dark, and then I'll scout out another way around."

They spent the rest of the afternoon back at the parking garage, munching on potato chips and other bags of junk food that Michael and Gabe had looted from the food court of the mall. The doors into that level of the mall weren't locked; like everything else from the days of Strain 7, everyone had been too busy dying or tending to the dying to turn off the lights and lock up when they went home.

Age didn't seem to have affected the snacks much. Keely ate most of the Crunchy Cheez Doodles, Michael was amused to note, devouring them with a look of ecstasy. "I really miss these," she said a little apologetically, "especially right before my period. Total salt cravings."

The usually unflappable Gabe looked embarrassed for the first time ever, and Michael had to hide a smile.

After a few hours of rest, at twilight they were back down to business. Gabe went on his own to survey the area for an hour and a half; when he came back, he announced that the soldiers were gone—there was no trace of them, except for tracks in the sand and dust where they had pulled away in their own jeep.

"But it looks like they're entrenched here for a while," he added. "They dug in a sort of base camp a quarter klick that way—there's something here they *want*. We should definitely go in on foot—easier hiding, and we're low on gas. We'll bring it in when we find the stuff we're looking for."

Just to be safe, the three of them took a longer way around, avoiding the technology park altogether. Right behind it, hidden from the rest of the city, was where the really ugly warehouse district began. One of them, flat and tan and at least an acre in size, had a flickering white sign out front that said Securasystems.

Michael gave a low whistle. "Would you look at that—it's still got power."

"More likely they made sure it *got* power recently, right?" Keely said. "This and the soldiers being here can't be a complete coincidence."

"You're right, Keels," Gabe said, sighing. "Why *wouldn't* they be interested in some of the last surplus of high-tech homeland security? So much for dropping in, hauling out the goods, and skipping merrily away."

"What do you mean? There's no soldiers guarding it," Keely said, looking through the opera glasses. "It's totally open and defenseless."

Michael almost cracked up. "And Novo Mundum chose *you* because *you're* the smart one."

Keely glared at him. "What's that supposed to— Oh. I get it," she realized, blushing. "A high-tech security systems company would probably have, uh, a high-tech security system protecting its warehouse of high-tech security systems."

"Let's go in for a closer look," Gabe said, though it sounded more like an order. "Hopefully you can use your magic keys to get us past whatever they have."

Michael wasn't sure whether to "sneak" or just walk normally; somehow Gabe managed to look both stealthy and alert at the same time. Keely trailed behind them, doing the same sort of look-around-and-duck thing he was doing. But there was no one around: the warehouse area was as dead as Jeremy's neighborhood. Tracks and oil in the dust indicated recent military presence, however.

They went to the back at Michael's suggestion; the lobby probably had two sets of doors, the inner door one that could only be opened from inside, by a receptionist or something. Next to the loading dock was a simple blue metal door, no window, no conventional lock, just a keypad with a card reader next to it.

"Thank God they don't have one of those retinal readers," Gabe said as Michael squinted, feeling around the edges of the plastic case that held the keypad. He found where it snapped to the wall and pried it open to look at the circuitry underneath.

"Would have been unlikely. It's not as common as movies make it seem—few companies are willing to take the risk of the possible eventual eye damage to potentially litigious employees. *This* is a very common reader, based on the TL-x2 system," Michael finally decided, relaxing a little. He pulled out his wallet and dug through the spare cards he always kept with him until he found a blue "administrator" skeleton key. "It's a common standard; my dad bought the company that invented it and then licensed the technology out to everyone else."

"Blah blah robble robble, but *can you open the door?*" Gabe asked.

"Pretty much." He traced the wires with his finger, frowning at some that went entirely the wrong way—*up* the outside of the wall, protected by a metal conduit. "What this does is lets us in for fifteen minutes; like if the night manager locks himself out, this gives him enough time to run in and punch in a deactivation code. If he doesn't do it, the backup alarm comes on and if any of the sensors are tripped, it sounds."

"Well, that could be worse," Gabe said, shrugging. "As long as we get away before the army notices."

"It also dead-bolts every door in the place," Michael added.

"So what you're saying is that we have fifteen minutes to get in, find the goods, get the goods, and get out or else we're *locked in,*" Gabe said, groaning.

"Yeah—but first we have to cut the power to the main door alarm." Michael frowned, following the wire up the side of the building. "I've never seen anything like this before—it looks like the door itself is on a separate circuit."

"So?" Gabe pulled a small hand ax out of his belt and indicated the conduit.

"No—it needs to be turned off manually," Michael said, waving his hands to stop Gabe from striking. "*Specifically* to stop people like you from doing something like that. Or if there's a fire or something and part of the door gets damaged, it calls the fire department."

"It looks like there's some sort of fuse box on the roof," Keely said, looking through the binoculars up at the building. "I guess someone will have to climb up there and flip a breaker or whatever."

Gabe and Michael looked at each other, then at Keely.

When she finally put the glasses down, she saw them staring at her. "Oh no—you want *me* to go up there?"

"Michael knows what this stuff we're getting looks like," Gabe said, shrugging, "and I'm speed and muscle. You're going unless you think you can grab a few fifty-pound boxes and all those locator disks and get out of there in fifteen minutes."

"Here's what we do," Michael said, thinking the plan out loud. Gabe and Keely listened politely to him—automatically accepting his expertise in this situation. Just like that. *Even the ex-soldier!* "Keely, you go up and throw the breaker. Give us a signal as soon as you do—whistle or something. I'll swipe the card and we'll go in. Gabe, you set your watch. After we go in, Keely, you run back and get the jeep and park it next to the lobby door—keep the lights off. If you hear anything or run into trouble, lead them *away from the warehouse.* If worst comes to absolute worst, Gabe and I can hide in there in a safe spot."

"Yeah, and then try again every hour on seven past the hour until it's safe for all of us," Gabe added, nodding. "Those soldiers could return at any moment. I think we're only going to get one chance at this, kids."

"All right?" Michael looked at the two of them.

"All right," Keely said, taking a deep breath.

Gabe grinned. "It's showtime, people!"

THIRTY-TWO

GABE AND MICHAEL GAVE KEELY A BOOST UP, PLAITING THEIR hands so she could climb to their shoulders, then reach over and grab the door frame. *I will not panic,* she told herself grimly. It was just like the climbing wall they went to on her thirteenth birthday. The tiny lintel on top of the door, the spotlight above it—each of these was as solid and wide a foothold as the rubber holds. Though her arms weren't that strong, once she grabbed either end of the vinyl siding, Keely was able to push herself up like a crab, one leg at a time, finding little toeholds. She threw her weight against the side of the building and did *not* look down.

When she'd climbed as far as she could, the flat roof was still just at her neckline. Keely tried to pull herself up onto it with her hands flat on the roof, but her upper-body strength just wasn't good enough.

She thought of Michael and Gabe below her and the people back at Novo Mundum. Gabe was a *soldier*—he regularly risked his life to protect them.

She couldn't let them down.

Closing her eyes for a moment and making a wish, Keely crouched as much as she could and *jumped*—

"Keely—" Michael gasped as she let go of the side of the building and leapt. Gabe didn't say anything, also watching openmouthed. She managed to throw her chest and her arms onto the roof, but for a horrifying second she just clung there, kicking her legs, trying to keep from sliding off.

Finally she was able to wiggle from side to side like a snake. She shuffled one agonizing inch at a time, but at last her head, body, and legs disappeared from view onto the rooftop.

"Holy cow," Michael breathed in relief.

"Aw, I knew she could do it," Gabe said. But his face was just regaining its color.

A minute or so later a stone flew over the side and landed at their feet.

"I think that's the signal," Gabe said. "You're on." He poised his finger over his watch.

Michael swiped the card. Gabe pressed the button. The door swung open, and they were in.

14:59 remaining

The hallway was pitch dark; there were no windows in the warehouse. Gabe had a big, old-fashioned torch-style flashlight, Michael a Mini Mag. There was a whiteboard on the wall of the back lobby next to the water cooler, with arrows and types of equipment drawn all over it like a football strategy.

"I think we should start in storage area B," Michael said slowly, willing himself not to be wrong, praying that what he read made the sort of sense he thought it did. Gabe nodded and they opened the double doors to the warehouse itself, which was as black as a cave and *felt* huge, though they could see nothing in it.

13:45

Gabe went ahead with the big flashlight, shining it in front of them and briefly up at the giant shelves and ends of the aisles, where signs hung, sometimes indicating the row and number of the aisle and sometimes plastered over with pictures of naked women cut out of old girly mags.

Their footsteps echoed and died against the solid cement floor—the place was *huge*. If they were wrong about where the boxes were . . .

"B," Gabe said, indicating a direction with his flashlight, up a flight of metal stairs that clung to the side of a wall.

Michael frowned. He was wasting precious seconds, but it didn't seem logical to store the heavy batteries, insulators, and other bulky gear for an electric fence where warehouse workers would have to haul it up a flight. A quick wave of his flashlight revealed benches along the catwalk, lined with smaller boxes. What looked like computer parts—and probably the GPS locator chips.

"I'll go up there," he said. "You look for the fence equipment. It should say something about high voltage on the box, be about this big." Michael indicated the size with his arms.

"Check," Gabe said, but he looked a little worried.

They split up.

11:35

Keely ran as fast as she could back to the garage, pumping her arms and legs like she used to in track, trying to remember the proper form. She kept the keys clenched in her fist, which was all bloody and scraped from when she leapt down from the roof to siding to the ground. It was one long tumble—her knees had gravel embedded in the skin from the landing and her pants were torn to shreds. That hadn't stopped her, though; she immediately took off.

Her lungs were on fire by the time she finally got to the garage; it took all of her effort to leap up the concrete steps two at a time. Two steps from collapsing, Keely had to hang on to the door of the jeep as she opened it—her legs were finally giving out. Her hands shook so hard that it took several times before she was able to get the key into the ignition.

"Damn!" she swore as she turned the ignition too hard, the starter echoing through the empty garage.

9:04

Michael ran down the narrow catwalk, scanning the neatly arranged pallets for the right box. *GPS handheld devices, GPS walkie-talkies . . .* If only they had more time and more people to help carry. This was a treasure trove of stuff Novo Mundum could desperately use. *Identification badges . . .* Locator disks!

Michael made himself take the time to stop and rip open a box. Neatly sealed in individual blister packs were tiny round disks, like flesh-colored UFOs. Five hundred per carton. After a moment's hesitation he reassured himself that they were solid-state technology and as delicately as he could dropped three boxes over the side of the rail.

7:23

Keely tried to coast as much as she could, engaging the engine only when necessary, in the lowest-possible gear. She had to stand up in the seat and drive with the tips of her fingers mostly; it was too dark to see more than a few feet ahead of the car.

She thanked her lucky stars as she made the final turn into the parking lot; no soldiers yet.

Then a figure leapt out into the road ahead of her.

4:20

Michael struggled with the boxes, carrying and kicking them toward the exit. They weren't heavy, just awkward. *Where's Gabe?* He started to back into the set of double doors that led into the lobby, intending to drag the boxes behind him . . . when he noticed a single red flashing LED on a card reader on the wall next to the door.

Why didn't I notice it on the way in?

Michael cursed himself and patted his pockets, trying

to find his wallet. He hadn't left it with Keely, had he? He *always* kept it in his back pocket. . . .

It was there, just pushed down far and he was panicking too much to have noticed it the first time. He pulled it out and started rifling through his security cards—half of them fell to the floor as he looked.

He cursed; even with his Mag light it was too dark to tell what different shades of pastel they were; he scooped them all up and began trying them one after another, swiping them through the reader and forcing himself to wait out the five-second reset between each try.

2:45

Keely backed up to the warehouse door, still shaken.

There was blood and flesh on the grille of the jeep. She put it in neutral, opened the door, leaned out, and vomited.

1:23

The second-to-last card worked. Michael kicked open the doors and grabbed the boxes, trying to plan what would happen if Gabe didn't make it out in time.

Just as he reached the outside door, though, the soldier came running up, pushing a dolly with several heavy boxes of industrial electrical fencing equipment on it. Gabe had been right about the weight of the equipment; it was obvious that even he couldn't have carried all of them.

Saying nothing, Michael stacked his boxes on top of the others and then ran ahead, pushing chairs and the watercooler and dead plants out of the way. He prayed the dolly would fit through the door—it looked like it would be close.

At one minute and counting, silent security lights came on, circling and strobing.

00:45

Keely tried to focus as the door of the warehouse flew open; Michael came through, pulling a dolly loaded with boxes. Gabe must be pushing from the other side. She checked her watch—it looked like they were going to make it!

But halfway through the door the dolly stuck, making shrieking grinding noises against the sides of the door.

00:37

"Help me!" Michael shouted as he reached up and started throwing the lighter boxes into the back of the jeep.

Keely wiped her mouth and climbed over the backseat; there were two big, heavy boxes left. She took one end and Michael took the other and she *pulled* as hard as she could, feeling the vertebrae on her spine struggle and creak.

00:09

The last box tumbled onto the backseat of the jeep—hopefully without crushing the locator disks beneath it.

Gabe grabbed the handle of the dolly and vaulted over it, red warning lights flashing behind him. He turned around and kicked the dolly as hard as he could, again and again with the tip of his boot, until finally it went flying backward and the door slammed shut.

At T – 0:03.

Keely drove off as quickly but as steadily as she could, Michael and Gabe grabbing onto the sides and leaping in.

"That was way too close," Michael said, shaking with adrenaline. *We did it, though!*

"Amen to that, brother," Gabe said. "Hey, what's that?"

Keely carefully steered around the body of a yearling deer that lay prone and bleeding in the parking lot.

"I thought it was a soldier," was all she said.

Her face was pale and her voice empty; Gabe and Michael looked at each other but didn't press further.

THIRTY-THREE

FOR THE FIRST TIME EVER, AMBER DIDN'T SHOW UP AT THE greenhouse for her evening shift. She asked Maya to tell Duke and the others that she had morning sickness, or cramps, or something else easily attributable to pregnancy. She wasn't exactly sure what probable symptoms were, but she figured Duke wouldn't know either.

She went straight to the security and information building, but her quick stride was soon slowed by a wave of heat or something that washed over her, like exhaustion, but nicer. She slowed down, wondering what stage this meant she was in *now*.

"Amber?"

She turned—it was some older dude; after a moment she realized he was Irene's dad. He'd already been here, waiting for Irene with her brother when the six of them had arrived. He looked a lot like Irene except that his dark curls were close-cropped and his eyes were a little lighter.

"You're Amber, right?" he huffed, having run to catch up with her. She nodded—this had better not take long. There were other things that had to be done. . . . "You were there when they took Irene, Jonah, and Diego away."

"I was getting a glass of water," Amber said defensively, suddenly feeling like she was being accused of something.

But he shook his head. "Have you heard from her? I thought maybe since you all seemed so close, you might have heard something. Quarantine can't be over yet, but I thought maybe . . ."

Mr. Irene was just a whacked-out, overly concerned parent. What could possibly happen to her at Novo Mundum?

Oh my God, she realized suddenly. I'm *going to be an overly concerned parent someday! Soon, actually.*

"No, but I'm sure she's fine," Amber said hesitantly, never having said anything like that before.

It seemed to work—the older man looked comforted. "Well, thanks anyway," he said. "Let me know if you hear anything."

Amber nodded, watching him walk off. *Having a baby = being a parent.* Soon she would have something in common with all of those older people . . . with her *mom. . . .*

She shook her head and continued to the building that was once the old computer lab. Guards similar to the ones who had prevented Dr. MacTavish from going into the research labs a few days ago stood aside when Amber sweetly told them a sort of version of the truth: that she had heard Jane was overwhelmed with computer work and was volunteering her own skills to help out.

She found Jane slumped over her computer, staring moodily at the screen.

"What do you want?" Jane asked, not even bothering to look up. "You can't send an e-mail to any of your family or friends or whatever, so if that's what you're after, you can just leave."

While she was a little taken aback by the woman's attitude—very *not* Novo Mundum—Amber also relaxed a little. At least she knew exactly where she stood with this woman.

"I heard you were completely swamped with computer work, so I thought I would offer my services," she said, trying to sound polite and educated.

"Oh yeah?" Jane looked her up and down skeptically. "You know Unix? Or Linux?"

Not even the words—but Amber kept that thought to herself. "No, but I'm a fast learner. I'm working at the gardens and I want to volunteer for extra work in the evenings, but no one wants me because they're worried about my, uh, *condition*."

She pooched out her belly a little. It had the desired effect: Jane's hard black eyes softened a bit.

"You're pregnant and you're trying to do *more* work?"

"I'm just so grateful you guys took me in, without

me even having been chosen by you," Amber said mournfully. The best lies always had a bit of the truth in them. "And I'm going to be out of commission for a little while after the baby is born, so I thought I would start making it up now."

Jane chewed the inside of her lip. Was she worrying about taking Amber on as an apprentice—or having someone watching over her shoulder to see if she was a spy?

"All right," she finally decided, turning back to the computer, conversation over. "Come back tomorrow at ten in the morning. But if you turn out to be a total idiot, I don't have time for you."

"Understood," Amber said, trying not to smile. She left, waddling a little more than she had to. *Me, an idiot. Not likely. I haven't survived the past five years by myself by being an* idiot.

And as far as she was concerned, it was a perfect situation. If she found out that Jane was the saboteur, she could expose her and be a hero. If not, well, Amber would be learning new skills and helping out Novo Mundum even more.

She smirked to herself, thinking of her old middle-school class. *If they only knew—Amber Polnieki, a* programmer.

THIRTY-FOUR

WHEN THEY MADE IT BACK TO THE GARAGE, GABE SUGGESTED they spend the night in the mall—after all, except for the soldiers there was no sign that there was anyone else in the city, and there were no windows in the building. Keely felt a little better—Gabe and Michael were high on their own success but managed to devote some of their attention to her, patting her on the back and telling her what a good job she'd done. But she had never killed anything before in her life, and while she wasn't a vegetarian, thinking about the poor deer—or worse, would-be soldier—made her sick.

The smell in the food court didn't help much, either.

"Hey, let's go into the Lord and Taylor," Michael

suggested. "Their bedding section. That would be a *great* place to spend the night!"

"Totally," Gabe agreed. "And that way, we can each have our *own* bed tonight."

"Great," Keely said, even though the word didn't quite cover the mixture of relief and . . . a little disappointment that she actually felt.

It was spooky the way their footsteps were muffled and their voices lost in the big, empty space. Keely only had to close her eyes to summon throngs of fat families and sullen teenagers, grannies at the Hallmark and kids at the Toys "R" Us. Bad music being played loudly and the murmuring echo of hundreds of people shopping. She opened her eyes quickly, the past too far away and sad to revisit for long.

They took some candles from the home decor section and set them up around the model beds. It actually looked romantic—especially since Keely chose a four-poster bed whose gauzy netting gave her some semblance of privacy without completely cutting her off from the other two. It was the bed she had always dreamed of as a kid, with a silk patchwork duvet and about a thousand goose down pillows.

"You all can take the first watch; I'm bushed," Michael said, throwing himself down on the king he had picked out.

"Thanks for the honor, Bishop," Gabe said. "But I don't think we need to worry *too* much." He had grabbed a couple of books from a Borders they had passed and sat cross-legged on the top of a child's bunk with an electric lantern. *Tom Clancy,* Keely noticed with a smile. *How appropriate.*

"I'm going to take a walk, I think." She was still too jumpy from the deer and the tension before, and being in the mall was bringing back a whole host of memories, some good, some not so good, many about Eric, many about Bree.

"You want me to go with you?" Gabe asked, looking down at her, concerned.

"Nah, I'll be fine. This is my element, remember?" She forced a smile. "Just want to get a little shopping done now that I'm here."

Keely wandered through the housewares until she got to an up escalator, then chided herself—it didn't matter anymore which way they originally went. *First floor, cosmetics and handbags.* And designer dresses, apparently. They must have been ramping up for some sort of fashion show before the virus really hit. Her big yellow flashlight randomly spotlighted hangers of shawls, cash registers, and ghostly mannequins in sequined dresses.

"All useless," she said aloud, moving her light over one mannequin that sported a drop-dead-gorgeous Morgane Le Fay gown of dark green velvet. She would have *died* for it or something like it just a few years ago—whether or not she had anyplace to wear it. One of her and her mom's few bonding things had been over thick seasonal *Vogue*'s and all the gorgeous clothes within.

She felt a surge of anger wash over her. The world had changed too much—*she* had changed too much.

Keely would have had no problem trading the stupid five-thousand-dollar gown for a single burger. The Manolo Blahniks for reliable hot water. The necklace for a single night free of grief over the past and worries about the future.

Running through a mall at night unrestricted should have been a dream come true.

She felt *old.*

Keely wandered away from the mannequin and over to the cosmetics. Maybe she'd find some high-end deodorant there; that was the only thing this floor offered that she and everyone else at Novo Mundum could really use.

Then she walked by the MAC counter. This made her smile a little; back in L.A., she'd never left the house without her favorite MAC lipstick in Viva Glam. She looked through the testers and found it, square tipped and half used by other eager teens. She started to clean the tip of it off with her thumb.

Wait—what am I doing?

With the first bit of whimsy she had felt in years, Keely climbed up over the side of the counter and dropped down the other, where salespeople once stood. She opened one of the sliding doors of the case and shone her flashlight inside. Hundreds of lipsticks. Untouched. In every color, neatly boxed.

Keely bent over and flipped through them until she came to Viva and took one. She felt a little guilty; Novo Mundum was all about sharing, *not* hoarding. She should take some back for everyone or none at all. She took another one and shoved it in her pocket, along with Bubbles, the stupid ugly frosted shade that Bree had liked—just because it was the same brand her big sister used.

She fingered the gold sunburst charm at her neck, the one she had given Bree and Bree had given back before she died.

Keely thought about how much fun the two of them would have had here—her little sister would have had no compunctions at all about taking as much makeup as they wanted and *not* sharing. *She* wouldn't have gotten caught up in how serious life had become.

Maybe Jeremy had been a little insane—but maybe he was also right about some things, like not completely forgetting the past.

"C'mon, Bree," Keely whispered, pushing back the tears. "Let's have a little fun."

When Gabe found her an hour later, Keely was wearing a little black dress, pumps, and a ridiculously huge black hat with a feather in it she knew Bree would have loved. She had carefully made up her face the way she used to and wore an amazingly tacky collar necklace shiny with topaz, huge cubic zirconia, and other things that weren't quite precious but sparkled dramatically in the flashlight.

"Uh . . ." was all Gabe said.

Keely blushed, taking off the hat.

"I was just . . ."

"Going on your shopping spree?"

"Remembering my sister." She turned the hat over

in her hands, spinning the soft felt against her fingers. "She would have liked this."

"I understand," Gabe said. There was an awkward pause between them. "I was just a little worried about you when you didn't come back after an hour. . . . You're *beautiful.*"

He kind of blurted it out, in a way that was totally unlike his usual flirting, confident self.

"What, this old thing?" Keely laughed. "I'll bet you say that to all the girls since 7 who manage to find dress-up clothes."

"No, I mean it, Keely—it's not just the dress. It's—" He came closer, not taking his eyes off her, as if she might disappear if he blinked. "I don't know. . . ." He shook his head and grinned. "We should find a matching pocketbook," he said, putting out his arm.

"Absolutely!" She smiled back and took his arm, and they walked over to the accessories section. "Something patent, I think. . . ."

"You were great today," he said, picking up a bag but not really looking at it. "I mean it. A lot of . . . *people* would have freaked out at climbing that building and going back by themselves to get the jeep."

"A lot of *girls,* you mean," Keely said, narrowing her eyes.

"No, I mean *people.* Civilians. City folk." He put his hand on hers and she looked up at him, into his face. "I mean it, Keels," he said quietly. "I was a little doubtful at first—but I'm glad you're on my team."

Keely flushed—it was probably one of the highest

compliments she had received since Strain 7. Before, people were always praising her for her looks or her PSAT scores and her brilliance and whatever—but no one had ever simply credited her with being *competent*. "Thanks," she whispered back. "That really means a lot to me, coming from you."

His deep brown eyes never leaving her own, Gabe leaned forward and kissed her.

Keely responded instantly, pressing herself into his arms. It had been a long time since *anyone* had embraced her—since she had let anyone. His lips were soft and he wasn't too aggressive; he just held her and kissed the outside of her lips. She felt loved, and sexy, and wanted—for the first time in years.

Since Eric, actually.

"No," she said, louder than she meant to, pushing Gabe away.

"I'm—I'm sorry, Keels," he said, meaning it. "I shouldn't have—it's just that—"

"It's not that—I just can't." *It's still too soon.*

"Okay. My bad. No harm done." Gabe forced a smile. "You're pretty irresistible in that outfit, though."

"I thought you said it *wasn't* the dress!" Keely accused him, relieved they were each dealing with it so well.

"Yeah, well, I lied. Normally you dress totally commune trash."

He offered her his arm again and she took it—taking a little patent clutch with her.

Neither of them saw Michael standing at the top of the escalator, just having come to look for them.

THIRTY-FIVE

MICHAEL WAS BACK SITTING ON THE BED HE HAD CHOSEN
when Gabe and Keely returned. When he'd seen them
kissing, he'd panicked in a way he hadn't in the warehouse. He hadn't known what to do for a second, and
finally he just spun on his heels and left. He wasn't sure
why; it just irritated him—what was Keely doing
dressed up in all of those stupid clothes? He thought
she was better than Maggie.

"Hey." Keely was dressed in pajamas now, with what
looked suspiciously like Kim Possible logos all over
them. Wow, talk about a blast from the past. The
chunky silver Rolex she wore—he was pretty sure it
was her dad's—stood out ridiculously against the soft
pink material.

"Don't worry, we brought you something too," Gabe said, throwing a Calvin Klein deodorant at him.

"This wouldn't be a bad place to live." Keely sighed, crawling into bed and hugging a pillow. "I'll bet there's flour and stuff in the food court—we could make pancakes. . . ."

"And what good would it do anyone if you lived here?" Michael prodded. "You'd be just another parasite, like Jeremy. Consuming without contributing to the new world."

Keely blinked in surprise. "I just meant it would be fun. . . ."

"Haven't you learned *anything* at Novo Mundum? And *you* were the 'smart one.' I'll take first watch."

He stomped off, unsure why he was upset. Out of the corner of his eye he saw Keely looking questioningly at Gabe—and Gabe looking uneasily after him.

The next morning when Michael woke up, Keely was forcibly cheerful, as if she was completely willing to chalk up his behavior the night before to random, posttrauma weirdness. Still choosing not to dig into the dried meat and fruit they'd packed with them, the three breakfasted on tiny boxes of sugary cereal Gabe had found in the drugstore and *Diet Coke.* In *bottles.*

"Holy Christ," Gabe said after he downed his. "I think I'd trade all of Novo Mundum for a case of this."

"You don't mean that," Michael accused.

"Nahhh." Gabe sobered up. "The things MacCauley had us do . . ."

"You were in the MacCauley army?" Keely asked, surprised. Michael had had no idea either. Gabe's face slipped from its usual good-natured easygoing look to something bleak.

"Briefly," was all he said. Then he shook his head and changed the subject. "We need to go get some more gas and fill the rest of the cans. Car Girl Keely, you want to do that with me?"

"I—I think Michael should come instead," she said quickly, trying to make it casual and failing. Michael looked at her in surprise. "You know better than we do what other things Dr. Slattery and Frank and those people might need—batteries and whatever. You can get those while we do this."

"Okay, Commander," Gabe said. He was smiling, but there was clear hurt in his eyes.

What's going on? Michael wondered. *Weren't the two of them sucking face just last night?*

He worried about how to get the pumps working all the way to the gas station. Didn't they need electricity to work? What were they going to do, knock them down and just open up the tank itself?

But when Keely stopped the jeep at an Exxon, she immediately went into the service area and came out with some tubing, as if she knew what she was doing.

"How is *that* going to help us with the pumps?"

"It's not," she said, indicating for him to drag the cans out. "It's going to let us siphon gas from these other cars. I don't think there's any way we can actually use the pumps, unless Frank told you something he didn't tell me."

"No—you're right." The words felt strange coming out of his mouth. And, he didn't want to admit it, but especially to a girl. Maggie was just about all the "girl" he'd had close contact with in the last couple of years and he was so used to just taking charge and making decisions, he sometimes forgot that other people were capable too. "I don't know how to siphon gas—I think I saw it on a sitcom once, but that was it."

"I do." Keely grinned, unscrewing the lid on the tank of an SUV.

"Oh yeah?" Michael said, smiling back. "What's an academic princess like you doing knowing things like that?"

"Remember when gas prices started to climb?"

"Yeah . . . *Oh*." He shook his head. "You Los Angelinos will do anything to get your gas fix."

"Hey, it's either this or empanadas."

Michael actually laughed—he couldn't *imagine* Liza or Maggie making a joke like that, but Keely really was one of the boys. *No*, he corrected himself. *Keely is just Keely, one of the regular* people. Even if she did kiss Gabe.

All of his irritation had dissipated by the time they got back to the mall, and except for one tense moment when they found evidence of the soldiers nearby— spent cartridges, boot prints in the dust—Michael and Keely were in high spirits.

Until they noticed that the mall's front doors had been smashed open.

Keely immediately put the jeep into neutral and

coasted it around into the garage, trying to make as little noise as possible. Gabe had given Michael the gun, figuring they would be more likely to run into trouble than he would. Keely grabbed her short bow, although she looked kind of silly sneaking into the mall with it. If Michael hadn't seen her at target practice, he would have laughed.

"What do we do?" she whispered.

"Go back to housewares first—that's where he would bring back the stuff he scavenged, I guess. . . ."

They crept through the food court again but soon realized they didn't have to worry about making much noise. There were shouts and laughter coming from the basement of Lord and Taylor. None of it sounded like Gabe.

Michael and Keely exchanged looks and continued down, stepping carefully and keeping to the back escalators.

They were halfway down the one leading to housewares when Michael caught sight of something that turned every inch of his face white.

Gabe was in a chair, hands tied behind his back with a pair of stockings, and blood was running down his cheek. Five men—some no more than boys—stood around him, kicking through the boxes of cereal, batteries, and radios he had found and laughing. Three of them were eating the pemmican like Slim Jims, as fast as they could shove it into their mouths.

"So tell me again," the leader began. He was raw and scarred, with a jarhead buzz cut and a long, uncombed beard. They must be survivalists—which was bad, but at least they weren't Slash. Two of them had guns. "Why are you here, soldier boy?"

"I'm *not* a soldier," Gabe repeated stolidly. "I'm from a small farm community north of here. I got sent down to get supplies."

"By yourself."

"Yes."

"Then where's your transportation? Or did you plan to *walk* 'up north' with all of this stuff?" The leader hung back for a moment, then nodded at another man closer to his age, who leaned over and backhanded Gabe so hard his head snapped around the other way.

Keely sucked in her breath, trying to keep herself from crying out.

"*Now* what do we do?" Michael whispered. How were they supposed to go up against five survivalists with guns?

"You can turn around and put your hands up," came a clear voice from behind them.

A MacCauley soldier stood there, semiautomatic trained neatly at Michael's spleen.

THIRTY-SIX

JONAH WAS BENT OVER, READING ONE OF THE BOOKS ON advanced geometry he had found at the library. The morning sun felt great on his back, even through the sweater he wore against the chill.

He *loved* taking his morning breaks on the green, in the middle of everything. Pots and pans were clanging, people were chatting or swearing—people waved as they walked by, calling him by name. He was still mostly shy, but their aggressive niceness was pleasantly wearing away at his walls. One girl had even invited him to a reading of her new poem. She was no Irene, but still . . .

"Jonah?"

He looked up from his book and saw Dr. Slattery standing over him, quietly amused by Jonah's rapt attention to the book. He must have been standing there for a few minutes.

"Dr. Slattery!" Jonah leapt up, closing the book immediately.

"Didn't mean to interrupt you," the older man said kindly. "What's that you're reading?" He turned his head sideways to look, and for some reason that little gesture set Jonah at ease—it was normal and *human.* "Wow, quite a lot for some light morning reading."

"I'm going to need it if I'm going to teach myself engineering," Jonah said, trying to sound casual but blushing.

"You are such an amazing self-starter," Dr. Slattery said with real appreciation. There was nothing patronizing or fake about it. "If only my daughter were as motivated," he added with a wry chuckle. Then he noticed something in the middle of Jonah's head and his brow furrowed. Jonah knew what Slattery was looking at—that area where his hair grew a little funny. . . . Jonah closed his eyes, praying the moment would pass. "That's a heck of a scar you got there—not very big, but deep. How'd you get it?"

Fell off the toilet when I was nine, standing on it to get my dad's aftershave out of the cabinet. It was what he always said.

"My dad slammed my head against the bureau when he was drunk once." He found the words coming despite himself, spilling out of their own volition. "I had broken his favorite Coke glass."

Dr. Slattery's face almost went white, but he composed himself. "That's terrible," he said quietly.

Jonah didn't say anything. He hadn't told anyone in years.

"It's amazing with what you've been through, what you still want to accomplish," the head of Novo Mundum began slowly. "That's actually why I'm here now. If you don't mind, we're going to throw a little extra workload on you—sorry, but you're being punished for how well you've done around here," he added with an apologetic smile.

Jonah was just relieved he had let the other subject drop. It was like he *knew*. . . . "Not a worry, Dr. Slattery. Whatever I can do to help."

The older man beamed. "*Excellent.* That's what I like hearing. We need to completely redo all of the water pipes in the research labs and no one has any idea how. Some of the rooms that have water now don't need it, and others need more, and of course, we want to use as little of the pump and generator as possible. Are you interested?"

"Absolutely, Dr. Slattery!" He was already letting him redesign a piping system?

"I'm upgrading your security clearance, so as soon as possible, you can start coming over to do research and check out the current layout. Thanks again, Jonah." He took the boy's hand in his own. "You're a very valuable asset to Novo Mundum."

Even after Slattery left, Jonah was still smiling. It was a few moments before he remembered the book under his arm and got back to reading it.

THIRTY-SEVEN

DIEGO CAME TO WOOZY AND SICK. IT WAS LIKE THIS EVERY time Nurse Chong brought him his antibiotics since he'd collapsed—he would pass out soon after getting the medicine and wake up violently ill. Somewhere, far in the back of his fevered mind, he remembered something vaguely about how people could be allergic to certain antibiotics. Nurses always asked when you had your checkups, when they filled out those forms.

Diego didn't want to go back to sleep again; in the days of Strain 7, if you went to bed sick, you probably didn't wake up again. He focused on the pain in his leg, the throbbing, and used it to cut a path through his fuzzy-headedness.

He was on some sort of make-do sickbed, what

looked like a lab bench with a thin cotton futon on it to make it more comfortable. Hadsn't Irene been here at some point? And someone else? What happened to them? He carefully sat up and swung his legs over the side, almost screaming at the pain. At least it woke him up.

His crutches were gone, but the benches were fairly close together; he pushed himself down off the side and balanced with one hand on each. On top of everything else, Diego was ravenous—he couldn't remember the last time he ate. But wait—wasn't being hungry a sign of health?

Without anything better to do, he decided to look for Irene, since his vague memories involved her in a lab-like room too.

Hobbling and hopping, he made his way out of the room, leaning on the wall. Old, yellowed cartoons that were only funny to geneticists and other scientists were tacked up here and there. Even in his addled state, Diego tried not to ruin them as he pushed himself along.

"Irene?" he called out.

She wasn't in the first room beyond his or the second one. He had to squint against the light from the windows; everything was hazy and a little blurry. He fought down a panic that he had been left here, forgotten. Like everyone else had evacuated the place and he was alone.

The third room had a huge safe-like door on the side that looked like it led into something that was a cross between a fridge and a safe. Someone had left it open a crack, and even though Diego knew intellectually that the room probably wasn't *cold*—there didn't seem to be any electricity on in this wing, at least not how—he couldn't overcome old habits and hobbled over to close it. *Kids could get trapped in there or something.*

As he pushed the door closed, he took a look inside, just out of curiosity. Instead of shelves of vials and test tubes and beakers and all sorts of other things he imagined would be in a laboratory's cold room, there were piles of grenades on the floor and big guns hanging from the walls—flamethrowers and rocket launchers and automatics and stuff.

"This should *definitely* be closed," Diego said aloud, echoing his nonnie.

Then he thought about it.

Didn't Frank tell them, at their first security meeting, that one of the reasons Novo Mundum was so vulnerable and depended on secrecy was because of their lack of high-powered weapons?

So why were they kept in the lab?

Nonnie might have been a bit more of a paranoid misanthrope than was strictly necessary even *before* Strain 7, but the result was that Diego didn't blindly trust anyone, not even a happy group of do-gooders like Novo Mundum. And Michael with his talk of spies . . . Something wasn't adding up. In Diego's experience of growing up in the extreme country, whenever there were people caching weapons, it was usually a bad sign.

But what should he do?

Tell Irene.

He turned around, but footsteps down the corridor made him head back to his room instead of trying to leave; somehow he didn't think that being caught in front of a secret pile of weapons was such a good idea.

Come to think of it, where *was* Irene and . . . who was it with her, Jonah? And that other girl?

Diego hauled himself up onto the bench with his makeshift bed, and just in time—Nurse Chong came shuffling around the corner with a hypodermic needle in her hand. "Hey, time for your antibiotics," she said chirpily.

"Another dose? Already?" Diego croaked, making it sound like he had just woken up.

"Lucky boy got extra antibiotics approved. Hey, did you get up or something?" she asked suspiciously, looking at his position in the "bed."

"No, ma'am," Diego answered politely. "I got hot and was trying to get the sheets off me is all."

The older woman just grunted as she pulled back his sleeve and readied the needle. He couldn't tell if she believed him or not.

Tell Irene about the weapons, tell Irene about the weapons, tell someone to tell Irene about the weapons, Diego told himself over and over again as the needle stung his flesh. He was probably going to pass out again soon, and it was imperative he remember when he woke up.

And somehow he just didn't trust Nurse Chong.

THIRTY-EIGHT

AMBER REPORTED FOR WORK AT JANE'S PROMPTLY AT TEN. JUST a few weeks ago she would have been nauseous from guzzling her food so fast, but now she was ravenous all the time and found even inedible things—like clover, for some reason—extremely enticing.

The tiny woman was slumped over her computer again, moony eyed, staring at the screen. When she saw Amber, she quickly hit send and alt-tabbed to another application. Then she sat up and put on her stern face and voice.

"Do you know anything about networking?"

"Only a little." *And by that I mean "nothing."*

Jane harrumphed. "For now go to that computer there"—she jerked her thumb over her shoulder—"and clear off *anything* that's not Office—Word, Excel, stuff like that are part of Office. *All* data files too. But just on drive C. Delete all the users and defrag the hard drive. I want the memory so clean I can eat off it."

"You want me to get rid of solitaire too?" Amber asked evenly.

"What?" Jane snapped, annoyed that she had *actually* been asked a *question.* "People shouldn't be using these computers to play games." Then she shrugged, eyes glazing for a moment, as if she was thinking of a happier time, when she was just one bored prog among many in some sort of computer firm. "I guess not. Leave it on. Too much bother. And when you're done, go to the help section and start teaching yourself about networking. Got that?"

Amber nodded and silently went over to the computer. She had no real idea what "defrag" was but figured she could find out about it through help or something. She learned fast. But first she went through each individual folder, laboriously deleting all the files that didn't look important. Sometimes she opened them up, but there was nothing really juicy except for a picture of an eight-hundred-pound naked woman that had been floating around the Internet for a while.

Jane left at ten-thirty to go "get some coffee"—she still insisted on calling it that, Amber noted with nasty amusement. Even though now it was mostly chicory root and a little bit of instant.

The moment she was out the door, Amber got up and slipped into her chair. The first thing she would do was check out that e-mail that Jane had sent so surreptitiously when Amber first came in.

In her sent folder there were messages to Dr. Slattery and Frank and other people at Novo Mundum, reports and updates on how the computer system was going. Amber was surprised that a computer and communications structure had survived this intact; in the greenhouses and the dorms they were pretty much cut off from the inner workings of Novo Mundum.

Aha.

But there, sent at 10:01 a.m., was a message to Tito Amurao—*at* a government institution! Amber quickly opened it.

And was just as quickly disappointed.

I miss you too—wish we could just talk sometimes. Everyone here is so stupid I want to kill myself. I miss your lips—and even your eyebrows! Are you still plucking them, or are they big and bushy like your dad's?

Amber stopped reading. If this was some sort of code, it was nothing she could crack. So Jane *was* a bit of a fraud—all by the book to others while breaking rules left and right herself. Just a dumb, lonely network engineer who didn't get along with other people.

And obviously disgruntled.

Maybe the letters to her husband were just a red herring—or maybe Jane was better at getting rid of all of her serious communiqués.

Amber would tell Michael when he got back and continue to keep an eye on her for now. It was kind of fun to be back at a keyboard.

Especially one with solitaire.

THIRTY-NINE

"ARMS ABOVE YOUR HEADS. NOW."

Keely and Michael raised their hands, unsure what else to do. The MacCauley soldier had spoken in a normal tone, but it was loud enough to cause the five survivalists torturing Gabe to look up.

"Friends of yours?" the soldier asked. He smirked, a bit like Gabe, Keely thought. *Not* evil. Just a person.

"No," Michael said. "We were just—"

"Everybody down. NOW!"

More soldiers appeared in the wide entrance that led to the rest of the mall, trapping Gabe and his captors between them and the soldier with Michael and Keely.

The leader of the survivalists, the one with the beard, raised his gun and fired.

"*Go to hell,* you fascist!" he bellowed.

The rest of his men followed suit, firing at the soldiers and ducking behind furniture. Gabe hit the floor and slunk off on his belly.

"Don't move," the soldier told Keely and Michael.

Then one of the survivalists turned around and fired at him. He braced himself and returned fire with his semiautomatic.

Keely nudged Michael and indicated the up escalator with her eyes. If Gabe was free, he would know to meet them by the jeep. Michael nodded. They waited another moment to make sure that "their" soldier was still occupied firing down at the survivalists, and then they took off.

Keely felt a sting on her arm as she ran, first cold and then burning. *A bullet,* she realized. *I've been hit.* But since it didn't affect her legs, she kept running after Michael, trying to ignore the searing pain. No one seemed to be following; from the shouting and screaming and bullets it sounded like both sides were far too occupied with each other to care about a couple of teenagers.

They made it to the food court without being followed. Gabe was already there, jogging with his hands still tied with the stocking. Michael ran ahead and held the garage doors open for them. Keely got into the driver's seat of the jeep without asking; Michael and Gabe jumped into the back. She ground her teeth and drove away, pushing through the pain as she turned the wheel.

Nobody followed.

Twenty minutes outside of St. Louis the three decided it was safe to pull over for a moment and regroup.

"Holy cow, that was screwed up," Gabe said, stretching, hands still bound with the taupe-colored knot.

"Hey, how did you get out anyway? Off the chair?" Keely asked. "It was like magic."

"Stupid hicks didn't tie me *to* the chair," Gabe said, rolling his eyes. "Now cut these things off me." Michael pulled out a knife.

"No, wait!" Keely cried. The two boys looked at her. "I mean, they could be used for other things if you don't ruin them. Like scrubbing, and filtering, and—what size are they, anyway?"

Gabe rolled his eyes, but Michael put the knife away. Keely leaned forward to pick at the knot with her fingernails, and the two guys' eyes widened with surprise and horror.

"Keely—your arm," Gabe said softly.

"Oh yeah." Keely realized her bicep was black with dried, cracking blood. She flexed her arm and it *hurt*. The initial panic and shock of escaping must have dulled it. She pulled up the sleeve and an ugly gouge showed where a surprising chunk of flesh had been ripped away.

"Just a glancing blow. There's no actual bullet," Gabe said. "We should bandage it up, but it's not serious. Just ugly."

"It's going to scar," she said mournfully. *Better than it getting infected like Diego's wound,* she told herself, but it was still upsetting. Not that she was as vain as she used to be, but still—*bullet* wounds? *And* her scraped knees and hands—she was a mess.

Michael took over undoing Gabe's hands. "We've got a little bit of antibiotic in the emergency kit Frank gave us. We'll bandage you up good as new. Man, Keely. If we hadn't seen it—I mean, you didn't complain at *all.*"

And I killed a deer thinking it was a soldier. I'm becoming a real survivor. Yippee skip. Here's to life after Strain 7.

"Aw, man!" Gabe said, shaking the blood back into his hands after Michael was done. "I cannot *believe* we lost all of those things I found—the batteries, the campers' butane, all those walkie-talkies. . . ."

"Hey, at least we still have this," Michael said, holding up his Calvin Klein deodorant and grinning. "And I think it's probably more important—at least for you two—than anything else back there."

The trip back was completely uneventful. Gabe even took over some of the driving—Michael volunteered, but there was no way Keely was going to let him learn how to drive, much less manual shift, on N.M.'s only jeep. She tried one more time to convince them to go back and get Jeremy, but Gabe and Michael were completely united in their refusal to even go back into the town of the dead and see "the little psycho."

"We can't bring him back," Gabe said cryptically.

They got home at dusk—just a little after, it became almost too dark to see. Fortunately scouts were waiting for them with candles to lead them in, helping to get the jeep on the raft and over the river. Although the three of them were exhausted, Michael insisted they "finish the mission." He was eager to drop the fencing equipment off first, but they decided to take the locator disks to Dr. MacTavish at the hospital so Keely's arm could be looked at, too.

People were already running around, gossiping about their return, and one or two cheered. Like they were heroes or something.

They made their way over to the hospital side of the research building like the three wise men, each carrying a box of the disks—though Michael took Keely's when she realized that her right arm had grown weak, like it was falling asleep or not getting enough blood.

Dr. MacTavish barely looked up from her textbook as they came in.

"We've got the locator disks," Michael said, putting them down in front of her. "And Keely got wounded. . . ."

Dr. MacTavish squinted at her arm, then shrugged. "Not the worst thing I've seen around here. We'll clean it up. I'll talk to Slattery about what to do with the disks tomorrow."

"Tomorrow?" Michael said, flabbergasted.

The doctor fixed him with narrowed dark eyes. "I'm

still not entirely convinced this is a good idea, medically or philosophically."

"I don't see how that's up to you," Michael said calmly. Keely had to give him credit for that; whereas the disgust was undisguisable on Gabe's face, his was politic and cold. "You can *talk* to whoever you want tomorrow, but I want mine in *tonight.*" He pulled up his sleeve and exposed his biceps. "Gabe? Keely?"

"I'm in," Gabe said, but she was pretty sure it was mainly out of loyalty to Michael and their mission and not any actual desire on the ex-soldier's part. Keely didn't say anything. She told herself it was because of the wound in her arm; no need to complicate things with additional surgery.

Dr. MacTavish sighed and shook her head. "You are a bunch of idiots," she said, pulling open a drawer with sterile knives soaking in bluish liquid—like what the combs used to soak in at salons. "You are so young and *stupid,*" she added, more to herself than them. Michael glared at her. Gabe just rolled his eyes and made an obscene sign while her back was turned. "Irene, get in here. We have some boobs who want their dog tags permanently attached."

"They're back?" a voice called from the other room. Things were quickly *clinked* down, like glassware or metal, and Irene came running in. Keely was surprised at how happy she was to see the other girl; they had only been gone two nights, but it felt like much, *much* longer. "Michael! Gabe! Keely! I'm *so* glad you came back all right!" She looked like she wanted to hug them, but between Michael's flexed arm and Dr. MacTavish glowering with a knife in her hand, the atmosphere didn't seem that amenable to displays of affection. "Uh, how can I help?" she asked instead.

"Prep them, incision on the upper arm. Clean the area with alcohol. You, get me out a couple of those disks," the doctor indicated.

Keely stood back as Gabe opened the box and two blister packs. She suddenly realized that he had noticed her reluctance and wasn't going to push the issue by taking out three. He was *extremely* perceptive and sensitive. . . . Keely focused on the disks. They were small and coated with some sort of beige, rubbery material—like the magnet she had to make Bixie swallow when he ate some scrap metal on the street. Tiny numbers were tattooed in pixels on the side, 420004 and 420005. Hers probably would have been 0006.

Irene swabbed the two boys' upper arms with a bleached piece of cotton dipped in alcohol. The doctor braced Michael with her bare left hand, neatly swiping open his skin with her gloved right hand. There was almost no blood. Irene sterilized one of the disks and handed it to her and she just sort of slid it under the skin, not down in deep as Keely thought she would. The whole procedure was over in three minutes.

"Go get a Band-Aid for him," the doctor ordered, taking a different sterile knife to Gabe. "You next?" she asked, indicating Keely with her chin.

"No, I'm worried about my arm—" She showed her the wound.

"We'll wait on you, then. There's a checkoff list somewhere that the Brothers Slattery came up with. . . . Irene, clean her and bandage her up. I have to go pretend to smoke a cigarette." When she was done with Gabe, the doctor got up and stomped out.

"Lovely bedside manner," Michael muttered.

"Oh my God, Keely, how did you do that?" Irene asked, touching the edges of the gouge tentatively.

"Bullet," Keely said, and she had to admit, it *did* sound kind of cool. The other girl dipped a larger piece of cotton in alcohol and began to dab at it, an apologetic look on her face when she knew it stung.

"I've got to tell you guys something," Irene said slowly as she worked, biting her lip. "I was quarantined with Jonah and Liza after Diego fainted. . . ."

"Liza? Is she okay?" Michael demanded, finally looking up from where his new disk sat under his skin like a jellyfish.

"She's fine—she misses you." Irene smiled wanly. "Diego just fainted, but he's not doing so well. . . . I'm really worried about him. Jonah and I came out of quarantine this morning and he didn't. . . ." She bit her lip.

Keely took one of Irene's hands with her good one. "I'm sure he'll be fine. He's not a quitter."

Irene sighed and finished disinfecting the wound. "Anyway, quarantine's between the research lab and medical, and while we were there, Dr. MacTavish came to visit us. I think she could get in using Diego as an excuse." She paused. "I saw her stealing supplies, Michael. From one of the other labs. One of Dr. *Slattery's* labs."

Keely sucked in her breath.

"Are you sure?" Michael asked. Irene nodded.

"I couldn't see exactly what it was, but I wonder . . . if she was trying to sabotage his experiments or something."

"You paranoid freaks were right," Gabe said with resignation and amazement. "I really didn't believe it before. But if he knew, why didn't Finch just tell us it was her?"

"We should tell Dr. Slattery and Frank immediately," Michael decided grimly.

"No, not yet," Irene said, winding gauze around Keely's arm. Keely felt strange, like she wasn't really participating in this conspiracy discussion—maybe she was weak from loss of blood, or pain, or something, but it felt a little unreal. Like things were happening beyond her control. "Let me get better evidence. . . . Judgment happens a little fast around here to be wrong. Let me see *what* she does with the supplies."

"She's right," Gabe agreed. "Y'all have other suspects too. Like Jane. And frankly, Ridley's always been a strange kind of malcontent."

"All right. But I think it's time we told Dr. Slattery and Frank *some*thing. They probably have a better idea than we do who the misfits here are," Michael said.

"I'm with you there. Let's talk to them now, when we bring the rest of the stuff over."

"Welcome home, guys," Irene said, with a lopsided grin.

All working together, they managed to haul the rest of the boxes over to Alumni Hall. The guards stood aside and actually saluted them; feeling her ego buoyed up, Keely began to see the draws of being a professional hero. Gabe saluted them back; Michael gave a nod.

Inside, another guard escorted them to Frank's office, where he and Dr. Slattery were meeting.

"Mission accomplished, sir," Gabe said to Frank. Keely noticed that Michael quietly let him take complete charge again; after all, Gabe outranked them. *How . . . mature,* she thought, surprised and unable to think of anyone else who would have ceded leadership and credit like that.

"Excellent work," Frank said with the closest thing to a smile Keely had ever seen.

"We managed to get about fifteen hundred locator disks and dropped them off with Dr. MacTavish. Bishop and I had ours done already." He held out his arm to show; Dr. Slattery looked it over with interest.

"Excellent! Tomorrow we'll calibrate the GPS software using you two as guinea pigs, if you don't mind," the leader of Novo Mundum said with a smile. Then he looked serious and somehow managed to look all three of them in the eyes. "You have done an amazing job. You're all exemplars to Novo Mundum."

Keely felt herself expanding under his gaze; *she* had actually taken part in something that had pleased and gotten her noticed by *Dr. Slattery.* Who had over a thousand other people to deal with!

"Thank you, sir," Gabe said formally.

"Well, I have to go now," Dr. Slattery apologized. "Time—and chicken faux-tisserie—wait for no one, and I skipped lunch today. Once again, great job, everyone."

On his way out he put an arm around Michael's shoulders, giving him a quick squeeze. "You did it, son. With this equipment and your ideas we'll have this place shipshape in no time. I'm sure Liza will be proud."

Keely caught the knowing look in the man's eyes; it was cute the way Michael almost exploded with relief and joy. It must be hard dating the daughter of the guy who ran the place—and it looked like he had just passed his first major hurdle.

When Michael finally recovered himself, he turned to Frank. "We'd . . . also like to talk to you about something a little less pleasant."

"Go ahead." Frank sat down again and clasped his hands, giving his full attention.

"Before Finch left, he said something about a spy or saboteur."

"What did he say?" the older man asked sharply, his gray-blue eyes narrowing in on Michael.

"Something about how the MacCauley soldiers who attacked us couldn't have known to come that way or found us without inside help. He didn't name anyone, but it sounded like he had suspected something for a while."

"Also, we found Finch's body," Gabe added. "Someone blew up him and the soldiers he was riding with using a rocket launcher or something."

Frank actually seemed to register emotion for a moment—upset, hurt, grief, it was hard to tell. *So he's not the cold jarhead we all thought he was,* Keely thought.

"I'll look into it immediately," the colonel decided.

"I have a hard time believing anyone here would be capable of doing something like that—especially since we don't have any heavy weaponry. But it's always a good idea to keep an eye out."

His complete confidence in the people of Novo Mundum was amazing. Even with the malcontents, like Jane and Dr. MacTavish. And maybe Ridley.

"In other news," he continued. "While you were gone, we almost finished rewiring the trip wires to be keyed to the fence rather than the old alert system and just began putting up the poles for the main fence itself. Next we have to start lining the old walls with the electric wire—if you have the software, we should be able to begin testing its efficacy tomorrow." Frank gave the closest thing he had to a smile, which was really just a thinning of his lips.

"What voltage have you decided on?"

"It's a toss-up right now. Paul wants to try that thing where you just pulse five thousand to stun them a little, confuse them until we get there. I think we should set our phasers to kill, as it were. Don't give 'em a chance to recover. But enough of all this: you boys—and girl, excuse me—must be exhausted. They're still chowing down in the dining hall, so head over there first. Oh, and we've turned on the water pumps in North Dorm just for you three—enjoy a nice hot shower after."

"Kick *ass*," Keely said before she could stop herself.

"See, there are advantages to being a soldier," Michael teased.

"All right, dismissed. But Michael—you see me in the morning about installing that software, okay?"

"Absolutely, sir."

Frank turned back to look at some paperwork and the three of them left, feeling a little giddy, a lot exhausted.

"I don't know, man—killing *everyone* who stumbles on us?" Gabe asked, shaking his head.

"Yeah, I kinda think that defeats the whole purpose of Novo Mundum," Keely agreed. "The evolution of the spirit of man, away from violence, on to peace."

"Well, that and someone's going to notice when troop after troop doesn't return," Gabe said, shrugging. "But peace is good too."

"I can see both sides," Michael said. "Bring it up at the next security meeting."

"Not me, I'm out." Keely grinned. "If you need a driver or a hero, that's one thing. The boring details and follow-through? No thanks. Back to teaching for me."

"Lazy ass," Gabe said as he pushed opened the door to the dining hall.

"Glory hog," Michael added.

And then the three of them stopped. The *entire* dining hall was standing, waiting for them. Then they all cheered.

Gabe, Michael, and Keely were then engulfed by a crowd of hundreds, all congratulating them and hip-hip-hooraying—and before they knew what was going on, they were hoisted up on shoulders and being paraded around the room.

Keely giggled and Gabe looked a little embarrassed, but Michael was definitely enjoying it.

FORTY

AMBER WATCHED KEELY BEING FORCIBLY CROWD-SURFED OVER the dining hall, looking vaguely embarrassed, and smiled to herself. It was bizarre actually missing her roomie—she had been by herself for so long that it had been a difficult adjustment in the beginning. Share and share alike at Novo Mundum aside, Amber was still a slob with the few things she had or kept, and Keely was a goody-goody who wanted to sleep as soon as lights were out.

She would have to wait awhile before saying hi and telling Michael about Jane—let them enjoy their kudos while they could. Besides, even the faux-tisserie special tonight was making her mouth water, and it was getting cold.

As Amber turned around to go back to her seat, she found herself staring right at Carter.

He had a tray in his hands and was just about to bring up his dirty plates and utensils, and the wide look of surprise on his face indicated that he hadn't realized she was there either. In this college dining room setting, he looked more like a dumb-ass student than the cool older guy she had once thought he was.

They were both silent for a moment.

"Hey," Amber said finally. "Surprise. I'm here too."

"Yeah," Carter said, clearing his throat and trying to sound casual. "I saw you when your, uh, group came in. I'm glad they let you in," he added. It sounded like a platitude, but his voice squeaked when he said it.

"Uh-huh," Amber said, a little sarcastically, but finally just *done.* This had been coming for a while, but whereas before she had been looking forward to the confrontation, now she just wanted it over ASAP.

He stared at her slightly rounded belly. "Is that . . . ?"

"Uh-huh," she said again, nodding slowly, like he was an idiot child, so he understood. "I'll be honest with you—I came here mostly to call you out. But that's all in the past. Live and let live. Consider it over, done, forgotten. *Everything* between us."

"Yeah?" He sounded hopeful, but it was a moment before he lifted his eyes from her belly to her face.

"Yeah, but I mean *every*thing." She narrowed her eyes and pointed at her stomach. "As far as you're concerned, your involvement ended the moment you took off. Got it?"

"Got it." He nodded quickly, infinitely relieved at this random escape from her, his guilt, and everything else. "I'm . . . I really am glad you're safe," he said, with just a little of the old sexy, in-control Carter she had fallen for. This was her moment to face him as an adult, peer to peer, making amends like in the movies.

"Whatever," Amber said instead, rolling her eyes and making a W with her two hands before turning away. Yeah, she was all about live and let live and maturity and all that . . .

But he was still a douche.

FORTY-ONE

HOLY GOD ABOVE, THAT FELT NICE, MICHAEL THOUGHT, walking back to his room with just a towel draped around his waist. God wasn't really part of Novo Mundum's doctrines—in fact, worship was kind of frowned on—but for once Michael didn't care. His body was still steaming from the hot shower, and he'd scrubbed and cleaned like he hadn't in ages. Like *new*. He hadn't even bothered to comb his hair yet, enjoying the just-scrubbed feel of it. Maybe he would even put on some of that new deodorant—he didn't feel really comfortable about using it in the day, when he was around other people, who didn't have any.

Michael was singing when he opened the door to his room—no one ever locked up—and was just about to whip off his towel to a particularly stirring refrain when he suddenly saw Liza sitting—no, *posing*—on his bed.

"Hey there, hero," she said, moving her shoulders so that her cleavage wobbled and insinuated itself around the silk bathrobe she wore—who knew where she'd gotten it. Her skin was rosy and warm, and his entire room smelled of her.

"Liza! I was wondering where you were." He sat on the bed next to her, marveling at her beauty: her red hair brassy in the rushlight and her wide, adoring eyes. He kissed her once on the lips quickly and pulled back to look at her again. "You look *amazing*."

She waggled her eyebrows suggestively, then let the whole kiss-me-you-fool thing drop. "I was so worried about you. . . ."

Michael felt something ease inside him as he pulled her close, like a tension that he hadn't even realized had taken root during his trip was just now finally letting go. Liza was smart and strong, but she still needed him, cared about him, and now he didn't have to worry about anything but just making her happy.

He leaned in and kissed her properly this time, pulling himself toward her with his arms around her back. *Down* her back, under her bathrobe.

They sighed into each other, skin to skin, and his heart started to race at the intensity of feeling her against him. Soon everything else faded until all that was left was just him and Liza and the flickering yellow light.

FORTY-TWO

It was dark all around him, and Diego couldn't remember what had happened to the day. He was finally out of pain—the wound must be healing. Although when he bent over to get a closer look, it didn't seem so good: clear liquids were oozing out the sides of the wound and ugly pink scar tissue was pulled back and cracking from the bloody, hard center of the bullet hole. For some reason, it didn't matter; he felt more optimistic than he had in days.

Like he was drunk, almost.

Wasn't he supposed to remember something? Something about Irene? It would be so nice if she visited. . . . A single one of her smiles would cure him faster; he was sure of it. She was so gorgeous and smart. . . .

He couldn't keep track of where he was anymore: it wasn't the dorm, it wasn't the hospital—it wasn't even the room he was in before he fell asleep. It looked like a waiting room, actually, or what was once a small office of some grad student peon or something. There was no one else around.

"Irene?" he called out tentatively, hoping against hope she was just around somewhere. He hadn't seen her since . . . well, since before he found the guns. *Guns!* He was supposed to tell her about the guns! He had to find her or get word to her somehow. Before she left, he had asked Nurse Chong where he was—she had patiently explained to him that the others were out of quarantine now, but he was still sick. . . . Irene would visit him, though, wouldn't she?

Things were getting a little too weird to be easily explained away. Novo Mundum wasn't that big and he wasn't that sick—Irene had said it herself. He didn't have the flu, just a bad reaction to the wound in his leg. . . .

His crutches rested against the wall; with some difficulty, he pushed himself off the gurney and grabbed them before falling over. The room was barely big enough for the wheeled metal bed; he had to push it aside with his hip to maneuver out the door.

It was time to get out. *That* much made sense through the fuzzy thoughts in his mind. He had to leave and find Irene, or Michael, or someone. . . .

This was a wing of the complex he didn't even recognize; the walls were a soft aqua and there were showers and eyewashes and other strange decontamination equipment up and down the hall. The floors were tiled and shiny, and silence echoed strangely off them as if Diego was the only one there.

Just like in a scary video game. He tried to dismiss the thought, chose a direction, and began to hobble down the corridor. He didn't get more than twenty feet before he heard something: whispers—murmurs—moans—

Diego tried to get a grip on himself, but this really *was* like being stuck in a lunatic asylum with zombies around every corner.

I should just keep walking, he told himself. He had other things to do.

But then someone or something let out a long wail, like it was in horrible pain. Diego *couldn't* just ignore it. "This place is a loony bin," he muttered to himself to keep his courage up.

He nearly tripped crutching around a corner; the huge, double-wide doorways suddenly seemed too small. Diego went on a little farther, realized the voices were fading, and doubled back, making a left instead of a right.

There were signs that people had been here: notebooks and computers that were merely sleeping, not off entirely. All sorts of laboratory, hospitally stuff. The air smelled of disinfectant, like it was cleaned fairly regularly and recently. He wrinkled his nose at the fake lemon scent.

The voices sounded louder again. . . . He turned through a room and then another room, both of which looked like his high-school labs, with tall taps and butane burners. He went through a door in the back and made a left, following the sounds, and found a wide hallway with a window set in the middle of it that looked down onto another room. The voices were coming from within.

Diego pushed himself up to the glass. It was hard to see anything at first; a red sun cast its dying rays from outside windows directly across from him, bathing the room below in a bright, sickly pink light. The way it reflected back onto the floor, Diego suddenly realized that what he was looking through was a one-way mirror.

He blinked and focused, trying to observe.

The long, narrow room was crammed with beds, some empty, some with people. Very, very sick people. Diego involuntarily backed away when he realized what he was looking at: the patients weren't African-American, as he'd originally thought—their skin was black from *sickness*. Limbs were swollen to unholy proportions or spindly like a spider's. Mouths like the slit mouths of mummies hung open.

"Water," one of the smaller patients cried. "I need water!"

Other patients groaned louder, as if stirred by this show of life and energy.

A door on the side of the room opened and Diego stepped back automatically before remembering that no one could see him.

Dr. Slattery entered, completely encased in a hazmat suit. Diego could see the man's face as he coolly scanned the room, taking in each patient in turn.

"Nurse Chong will be right in," the doctor said.

"Please . . ." One of the patients put her hands out to him. Sheets of skin sloughed off as she moved, falling from her arms like she was decaying on the spot.

Diego fell back, gagging. A wave of dizziness swept over him and he crashed to the floor.

He couldn't get up.

The shadows changed above him as the sun slowly set. Little silver things appeared at the edges of his eyes when he opened them, so he kept them shut. *People who went to bed with Strain 7 never woke up.* The next time he opened his eyes, it was dark.

"You shouldn't be here," came a stern but kindly voice above him. Chong?

"Well, that settles it," another voice said, resigned but determined. Was it Colonel Frank's? "He's *definitely* going to Paul now."

What did that mean—going to Paul? And why did Frank sound so sad?

FORTY-THREE

Liza admired Michael as he put on the old polo he tended to wear, buttoning it up while straightening out his neck as if he still lived in the world of starched collars and board meetings. He looked very serious as he did it and ran a hand through his short blond hair several times before she gave him her brush.

"I'd kill for some gel," he admitted, sighing.

"You should have taken some when you were out in the wide world," Liza said, hands on her hips. "And gotten me some blue jeans, too—just like in communist Russia."

Michael opened his mouth to say something but at the last minute seemed to change his mind. Liza frowned. Had she gotten the part about Russia wrong?

Or had something else happened at the mall where he, Gabe, and Keely had spent the night—something he didn't want to talk about?

"I'll head out with you," she decided, pulling her own shirt over her head. "I have to do some . . . clerical work for Uncle Frank, anyway."

Michael grinned at her, knowing it was a lie and immensely enjoying the attention.

"You two seem pretty close," he said, opening the door for her.

Liza shrugged. "After my mom died, my dad buried himself in his work. Total textbook case of it. Uncle Frank took care of me and let me cry and stuff. . . ." She shrugged again; that time was over and gone. Not worth talking about. Maybe someday, with Michael . . . But not now. "He's always sort of taken care of me. I mean, Dad's great and all, but with his research and the other books he published . . . Uncle Frank is easier to talk to about some things—he's always understood me, I think better than Daddy."

They actually held hands on the way over; even though the morning was crisp to the point of cold, a yellow sun shone in a blue sky and it really felt like they were at the beginning of a new world. People waved to them as they happily worked, fixing, harvesting, weaving, teaching.

"'O brave new world that has such people in't.'" She sighed.

"What's that?" Michael asked, squeezing her hand.

"It's from *The Tempest,* dummy. By *Shakespeare?*"

"Sorry, faculty brat." He smiled, squeezing her hand back. "I was *just* looking at colleges when Strain 7 hit. Some of us didn't have the advantage of growing up at a university."

"College," Liza corrected, but halfheartedly. Just another thing that separated her from the rest of the Novo Mundians . . . being here first. She would probably never completely fit in.

No one noticed or questioned her presence when she slipped into the room behind Michael and found some paperwork to pretend to be busy with. Fortunately, that busybody Jane was bothering some-one else some*where* else; Liza could watch, virtually unnoticed, from behind the metal shelving that sepa-rated the two areas.

Gabe and Uncle Frank were already there, waiting— Gabe trying not to smirk at the couple. Michael ignored him and went right to the computer. The hardware for the electric fence and its related software sat neatly nearby, unpacked and ready to go.

And, far more importantly, Keely was nowhere to be found.

"We didn't touch nothin'," Gabe said.

"I think Jane could probably have installed it, but we wanted to wait for the expert," Frank added.

Michael nodded, picked up the boxy metal thing, put a tiny screwdriver in his mouth, then threw himself under the table to get at the computer. "Where is the main electric line to the fence going to come in?"

"We have it installed already, here." Frank sat back

as Gabe got down on his knees and handed the end of a brightly colored insulated wire to Michael. "Power's connected to the energizer too, so be careful."

Trying not to let her foot tap, Liza actually started to work, copying documents. At this point she was cheaper than a mimeograph. *Daddy should see Michael now.* He looked so determined and smart—like a computer geek without the geek part. Her dad definitely seemed impressed with the outcome of the mission, and Michael obviously really liked him—the two men would get along so well. . . . Liza just wanted to speed things up a little.

Eventually Michael was done with whatever mechanical fiddling he needed to do and started to install the software and drivers while Gabe brushed the dust out of his hair.

"For now, unfortunately, we need two *separate* programs," Michael explained. "A topological- or map-style program for tracking the locator disks and the other one that came with the fence. That one controls it, tracks the power usage, lets us know when someone has tripped the fence and where, and allows us to vary the voltage."

"The Perry program," Frank said wisely, nodding.

Gabe, Liza, and Michael all looked at him.

"Perimeter. *Perry.* The Perry program," the older man explained, as if it was the most obvious thing in the world.

"Right. The Perry program," Michael continued. Liza smiled to herself. Sometimes she thought that Uncle Frank really had spent a little too much time with the army. "In the best of all possible worlds, we would combine the programs—maybe we can get Jane to work on that later—so we can track everyone *and* keep an eye on the perimeter at the same time, to warn people if they get too close, especially the kids."

"That would be totally cool," Gabe said, nodding. "We could eventually make the perimeter complicated and random, like in a video game—like *we* would know the right places to step, but an outsider wouldn't."

"Unfortunately, that would require feedback devices on everyone as well," Michael answered, shaking his head. "It's a good idea, but right now we have no way for people with locator disks to know exactly where *they* are in relation to everything else—only someone at the computer would know that."

"Well, when people are working on the fence and we test it, there should be some way of knowing who's close to it so we can warn them away when we go live," Frank said, worried.

"For now I can draw an approximate line on the top-ographical map program as to where the fence is." Michael pointed at the screen, where he was calling up a top-down map of Novo Mundum and its environs. It was a little old, Liza noted; roads and buildings that had been constructed on the old Greenwich College campus weren't reflected in the lines and boxes on the computer. "Starting this morning we can use people with locator disks already installed—like me and Gabe—to stand at either end of each new section of the fence, and you can get our coordinates and mark them on the topo map as the beginning and end of that part. It will be accurate to within a foot under open sky and eight feet under trees."

Frank snorted. "That's a hell of a margin of error."

"Well, if an enemy trips over it, the . . . Perry program can let us know *exactly* where it happened. That's why we need *both* programs."

Frank left the room, muttering something about getting a cup of coffee and how stupid computers were. Michael looked over to Liza and they traded a smile—it might not seem like it, but her uncle was very impressed with him too.

FORTY-FOUR

AT FIRST AMBER WASN'T THRILLED TO BE IN ONE OF THE FIRST groups chosen randomly to get a chip inserted; while she knew it would help protect Novo Mundum, it was still some sort of man-made thing that they were going to inject into her body. Which was currently dealing with a *girl*-made thing inside right now, thank you very much.

But as she got closer to the clinic, Amber remembered the first time she went there for a checkup right after she, Keely, Irene, Diego, Michael, and Jonah just arrived. That was when they *proved* that she was pregnant. Nurse Chong and everyone—even Dr. MacTavish—were really excited. They cooed over her and congratulated her and made her feel *special.*

There was a line in the old waiting room, but it was moving

quickly, and everyone insisted that she sit down, that she should go first, that she should put her feet up. Treatment she wouldn't have gotten in the urban, pre–Strain 7 world, where pregnant teenagers were a dime a dozen.

"Next," came a weary voice.

When it was her turn, Amber was pleased to see that it was Irene doing most of the prep work and often the procedure itself as Dr. MacTavish went in and out checking on more serious patients.

"Hey," she said, extending her arm.

"Amber! You look *beautiful,*" Irene said, eyes widening. "Radiant, just like they say."

Amber grinned.

Nurse Chong came in, her distinctive pigeon-toed step announcing her presence before they saw her smiling face. "Ms. Polnieki! You *do* look great." She looked into the waiting room behind the two girls; there were only a few people left. "Could you guys come back in, like, fifteen minutes? I want to give our new mother here more of an exam."

Without a grumble, *pleasantly* even, like everything at Novo Mundum, they filed out, murmuring words of congratulations.

"Take her blood pressure," the nurse told Irene, getting out a stethoscope and putting the earpieces in. She rubbed the diaphragm between her hands to warm it up, a touch that wasn't lost on Amber. When it was pressed against her belly, there was no shock at all. The blood pressure cuff expanded on her arm, but she barely noticed, practically kicking her legs in anticipation at what Chong might be hearing.

"One thirty over eighty-five, a little above normal," Irene said, unsticking the cuff. "You're probably just nervous."

Nurse Chong was grinning. "Here," she said, holding out the earpieces. Amber practically tore them out of her hands.

At first all she could hear was her own stomach gurgling and her heavy heartbeat. But after a moment she noticed a much softer, faster rhythm, like someone was tapping on a tiny bongo. *Dum-dum-dum-dum.*

"Oh my God! Is that her?" Amber asked, eyes widening.

"Him or her, who knows?" Chong shrugged, but she was grinning. "Yep, you're between four and five months—the quickening, some call it. You can feel it moving now, right? And no more morning sickness?"

Amber nodded, still listening.

"Can—can I hear?" Irene asked shyly. Amber looked at her in surprise, then took out the earpieces and handed them to her. The other girl frowned, and then her face lit up.

"That's *amazing,*" she murmured.

"We need to get you a labor partner," Chong said, *tchk*ing her tongue. "The dad isn't here, right?"

"He's . . . long gone," Amber said slowly.

"I'll be your coach," Irene volunteered.

"Yeah?" She looked at the other girl in surprise. Amber never really thought that the two of them had anything in common—even Keely was more old school and street-smart than Irene. Irene was the nice one, bound for medical school, the perfect daughter, sister, friend, Girl Scout, whatever.

Labor coach, maybe.

"Absolutely!" Amber decided. It was strange letting someone else in like this, and maybe she would regret it later, but for now it seemed like the right thing to do.

"I have to go help Dr. Slattery now," Chong said to Irene. "You think you can continue with the procedures for a while?"

Irene nodded, but the nurse barely waited for an answer, toddling off again.

"Well, now the fun part's over." She sighed. "I have to cut you now."

"Whatever." Amber held out her arm. "Hey, are you in on this whole sabotage thing?" she pressed as soon as the nurse was out of the room.

"Yeah, Michael has me keeping an eye on MacTavish. He saw her trying to bully her way into the research building. And then *I* saw her stealing supplies from one of Dr. Slattery's labs inside. But we're not doing anything yet. . . ."

"I'm watching Jane. I don't know if she's a traitor, but she's *definitely* a dork."

Irene smiled wanly as she sliced open Amber's arm.

"Hey, is something wrong?" Amber asked.

"Diego didn't come out of quarantine with the rest of us," Irene said slowly. "And he's still not out. I don't know—I hope he's . . ."

"Weren't you all yelling about how it wasn't a disease, just his infection?"

"Right—I don't know if he's too weak to be moved anymore, or if he really does have something, or . . . No one's told me *anything*."

"Not even your best bud, Dr. M.?"

"She doesn't know. If I can even believe her about anything anymore. Chong says he's fine, but Slattery's handling him now because Dr. MacTavish doesn't have a solid background in, uh, real medicine."

"I know. Dermatology—right? At least she'll be able to patch him up so he won't scar after."

"They don't want me to worry. I think they have me doing *this*"—she indicated the disk as she slipped it beneath her skin—"to keep me busy."

Amber snorted. "They have you doing 'this' because you're the only one who can do it besides them. So why don't you just go find Diego for yourself and see how he is?"

Irene shrugged. "Quarantine separates the hospital from the research side of the building. In fact, it's the only way back and forth on the inside. Diego's on the *other* side. And often if Dr. Slattery is in the middle of a really dangerous experiment, he posts guards there. And *no* one goes in or out of the research labs without serious business. Or permission from Slattery."

"So?" Sometimes Amber really didn't understand these other kids. Maybe too much education drained your common sense. They were so . . . *timid,* making problems where there weren't any. "*You're* serious business. You're one of the closest things to another doctor. And somehow Dr. M. got in, right? Put on your doctor gear and *go.*"

"I don't know. . . ." Irene tensed and untensed her hands.

"You haven't been told precisely you *couldn't,* right? Look, I would never do anything to hurt Novo Mundum, and neither would you—the rules they have are to keep the rest of us unscientific types safe. But you know what you're doing and how to avoid getting a disease, and if they catch you, big whoop. You can tell them the truth. You were worried about Diego. There's nothing wrong with that."

A faint ray of hope lit up Irene's face. "Maybe . . . maybe I will," she said slowly.

This might be a pretty good partnership after all, Amber decided. *She coaches me in pregnancy stuff and I help her grow a backbone.*

FORTY-FIVE

IT TOOK A LOT LONGER THAN ANYONE THOUGHT TO GET THE
software running; the sun had set before Michael managed to get both the Perry program and the Topo GPS
programs so both could work at the same time. Liza
had ducked out during dinner and brought him back a
sandwich wrapped in a cloth napkin, which caused
Gabe to shake his head. "No one does *jack* for Gabe,"
he said mournfully. Frank rolled his eyes.

"I'll make sure you get a doggy biscuit, soldier. I
know it was *real tough* sitting inside all day watching
your friend work."

"Hey, if I knew computers, I'd help."

Michael took a huge bite of the sandwich and looked
around for Liza, but she must have slipped back to the

desk behind the shelves and continued working. Unlike Maggie, who would have been bothering him for attention every five minutes.

"Can I ask you *ladies* to do one more thing before you call it quits?"

It had taken Michael a while to get used to the older man's way of speaking, but now he could see the pride in his eyes and ignored the spoken insults. "I'd like to map out one section of the fencing. Do that thing you were talking about to locate it on the topographic program. I'm not going to feel comfortable about letting any civilians near this little electrocution machine until we can warn them away."

"Sir." Michael spoke politely, try to hide the weariness in his voice. "It would be easier to do in daylight. We can just leave the power disconnected until tomorrow so there aren't any accidents."

"Humor an old man," Frank said with a face. "And that's an order."

"Yes, sir," Michael said, trying to hide a sigh. He took another huge bite of sandwich and passed it over to Gabe, and the two headed out into the night.

Liza watched them go. Maybe she'd give Michael a second "welcome home" later, but there really was a surprising amount of paperwork to do. She smiled when Uncle Frank sat in front of the computer and began playing with things. For an old guy—fifteen years older than her dad—he had really kept up with technology. Computers were just like cars, he said, except that you didn't have to get down on your back to tinker with them. Whenever she had a problem with the Web or Word or AIM or something, Uncle Frank was always the one who fixed it. He even played video games—not first-person shooters, but complicated ones like Warcraft and Age of Empires.

As he clicked around with the mouse and typed at the keyboard, numbers appeared at the top of the screen. Two little dots blinked their way across a computer-drawn landscape. The typing stopped for a moment as Uncle Frank looked at them, but then he began again, making comforting little clickety noises while Liza worked.

The evening was damp in some places and wet in others; things got dark a lot faster under the pines than back at the open campus of Novo Mundum. Michael and Gabe saw several tired sets of workers coming back from working on the fence who waved a pleased but weary hello. They followed their paths back over the crushed leaves to the most recently worked on part of the fence.

"There are two separate pieces of it here; it's going to make things difficult." Gabe sighed. "They've run an eventually live wire through the chain-link fence itself—"

"That's retarded," Michael interrupted. "By definition the fence is *grounded,* so it's just going to short the whole system."

"No, look here, genius boy." Gabe pointed out tiny plastic guides, like cogs from a cheap kid's watch, that held the near-invisible wire away from the fence itself.

"So what's the point? What are the chances someone's going to put their hands *right there?*"

"Well, that's what the trip wires are for, dill hole." Gabe turned on his tiny flashlight and began shining it back and forth along the forest floor. "I guess there's eventually going to be a maze of them."

"Let's just get the coordinates on those first and deal with the rest of it later," Michael said, surprised how exhaustion had finally made him begin to snap. For heaven's sake—hadn't he just come back from a three-day expedition with soldiers, and death, and little psycho boys? Couldn't this wait until tomorrow? He surprised himself, never having questioned any orders at N.M. before. *But really, it doesn't make a lot of sense. . . .* "When we find the two ends of each section, we'll each stand at one end for, say, a minute. Then we can go back to the computer and track our path."

"Well, I guess the good news is that the trip wire is impossible to see," Gabe muttered. "I—"

There was a flash.

Michael's subconscious recognized what it was before his conscious mind would accept it. The same sort of flash when a rat touched the third rail in subway tunnels. Blue and explosive, with a terrible pop.

He turned his own flashlight toward the noise, eyes taking a moment to adjust after the fireworks faded from his eyes. When it was obvious Gabe wasn't still standing there, he trained the beam on the ground.

"Gabe?" he asked, hoarsely.

There. Sprawled, eyes wide open. Black and charred where his shins had hit the trip wire.

And no movement.

FORTY-SIX

IRENE WAS SHAKING AS SHE CARRIED A RACK OF TEST TUBES UP TO the front door of the research building. She had tried going inside, through quarantine, but there were often guards on the other side now, and she'd chickened out. The two guards at the *outside* door didn't even look at her until she was within a few feet. The test tubes were filled with colored water and powder and other important-looking chemicals.

"These are supposed to go to the lab," she said, trying to hold them up without spilling anything.

The guard on the right looked her over once and then lost interest. "Go in," he ordered.

As she stepped over the lintel, Irene was positive she was going to have a heart attack. But nothing happened, no alarms went off, no one tried to stop her. Maybe Dr. MacTavish was the only one for whom this was really off-limits—because she was a troublemaker.

Irene ditched the tray of test tubes in the first likely room and made for the second floor—the one where the real viral research was being done, where the quarantine rooms divided the labs from the hospital side of the building. She found a surgical mask and gloves and put them on, trying not to think about Dr. Slattery in his full haz-mat suit. Very few things were actually contractible from skin contact, she told herself. Dr. MacTavish herself had worn the bare minimum—and she should know better than anyone else what you could get from skin contact.

Upstairs Irene had one horrifying moment as a lab assistant passed her in the hall: he was dressed much like her, in a mask and gloves, but wore an apron as well. All he did was nod at her and maybe smile as he passed; his eyes crinkled up at the edges, but the mask covered his mouth.

She finally made it to the quarantine area, figuring that if Diego wasn't in there, then at least he'd be close by. *No guards on the research lab side!* She could have just walked in from the hospital side if she hadn't been so scared. *Or such a wuss,* as Amber would say. She found Diego in a tiny room, more like an office than anything else, lying on a gurney that took up most of it.

His hands were tied to the sides.

"Diego?" she asked softly, pulling the mask off.

"Irene?" His eyes slowly opened—the pupils were

huge, and the skin seemed limp around his face. "Are you really here, or is this another dream?"

"It's really me," she whispered, reaching out and stroking the side of his cheek. Irene was torn, though; the chart on the end of his bed looked like it had been recently filled out and she was dying to see what it said.

"Irene!" He tried to sit up quickly and was brought up short by his restraints. "Irene, there's a whole cache of really big guns and weapons in one of the labs—like rocket launchers and stuff. The kind they said they didn't have! And there's other people here, somewhere, who are so sick—like with the plague. You've got to help them!"

"Shhh, what are you talking about?" she cooed. His forehead was damp with sweat, but he wasn't feverish.

"Their faces were black. It was *horrible.* And Dr. Slattery was there. . . ."

"You've been dreaming, Diego. It's okay. It's all over now."

"*No,* Irene, it's not." He lifted up as far as he could and looked her directly in the eye. "I *have* been dreaming, but I know I'm awake now, and I know I was awake then. Somewhere in this building is a room full of really sick people, diseased. I found it when I was trying to get out to tell you about the guns."

Irene's head whirled as she tried to make sense of what he was saying. "Slow down—what people?"

"They were in beds, jammed together. I passed out. Irene, something *weird* is going on. Promise me you'll look for them. Tell Michael about them and the guns. It's important! *Promise.*"

"I will," Irene said, watching the color fade from his

face again. Just that little bit of talking had taken all of his energy. She stroked his hair back from his forehead and when he was asleep, breathing peacefully, she carefully unhitched her other hand from his and went down to look first at his wound. The area where the bullet had gone in still looked bad and more inflamed than it should have been, but it wasn't the ugliest thing she had seen in a textbook.

His chart was actually far more interesting.

The last note on it was from a few days ago, the day when he was taken out of the quarantine room with her, Liza, and Jonah.

Stop all antibiotic. "No heroic measures." Skip October. Ennea.

No further help. So was this it? Had they given up on him? Or was he healing enough for them just let his natural immune system take over? "Skip October"? What did that mean? And there was that word, *ennea* or *enea* or whatever.

As she put the chart back down, she saw an empty vial on the floor, a cartridge for a needle. She picked it up and had started to look at it when there were footsteps down the hall. Irene shoved it in her pocket to look at later. There was no escaping; whoever it was would see her the moment she tried to leave the room.

What would Amber do?

Lie, of course. And act cute.

Irene fixed herself next to Diego again and was holding his hand and looking moonily into his closed eyes when Nurse Chong turned the corner.

"What are you doing here?" the older woman asked in the coldest tone Irene had ever heard her use. Like they were complete strangers.

"I was worried about him," Irene said mournfully. "I missed him."

Chong glared at her but asked no further questions—apparently she wasn't going to question *how* Irene got in. "You shouldn't be in the quarantine wing. This is for patients and health care workers only. *And* you should be spending your time putting in those disks."

"I'm sorry, you're right," Irene said, putting on an appropriately chastised face. "Are you going to give him his antibiotic shot now?"

For a moment Chong looked unsure. "Yes. Why?"

"Can I administer it?"

"Absolutely not. Slattery would have my hide if something went wrong, and by the looks of it, you're breaking the doctor-patient barrier here."

Irene sighed. "Yes, ma'am."

"Please don't come back here unless I say it's okay," the nurse said, biting her lip and looking a little more human. "It's really not safe with Dr. Slattery's experiments."

Irene nodded and slunk out.

She made a halfhearted attempt to look for the "room of sick people" Diego had been talking about, but once she pulled the vial out of her pocket and got a good look at it, Irene gave up. *Phenobarbital?* Happy juice. No wonder he was seeing things and looped out of his mind.

But why were they giving it to him instead of the

antibiotic? Why waste the painkiller on someone who probably didn't need it? And most of all, why was Nurse Chong *lying* to her?

At the last second Irene turned and went into the lab where she had seen the notebooks and files two days before. Making as little noise as possible, she opened the old dark green filing cabinet and flipped through the files until she found *Sandoval, Diego*. There was also a file labeled *The October Project->Ennea*, which she grabbed as well.

She went back out the way she came, hiding the files under her shirt. *But how long will it take before someone notices they're gone?*

FORTY-SEVEN

"GABE!" MICHAEL CRIED. OPPOSING THOUGHTS TORE AT HIS mind:

There is no way the fence could have been turned on.

And:

I'd better not rush over to him; the wire could still be live.

Hating himself, Michael took the time to locate the evil, nearly invisible gray wire that his friend had tripped on and tossed a branch at it. Nothing happened—it was already off again. But he still carefully stepped over it when he went over to his friend. Still warm; weird, shallow breathing. Weird, irregular heartbeat. As tired as he was, Michael bent over and slung the ex-soldier over his shoulder.

Why didn't we bring radios with us? He staggered through the bushes, trying not to flinch as wet branches slapped his face. He could *not* give up now. No. If he could just make it to the clearing . . .

"Help me!" he cried hoarsely, hoping someone would hear. "Help—I've got to get him to the hospital!"

Bless Novo Mundum. Without asking any questions, two people ran up to him, a man and a woman. They carefully took Gabe's torso and legs and hoisted him away at a trot to the clinic. Michael jogged behind. They made a strange procession across the otherwise peaceful dusk campus.

Inside the double doors of the hospital everything was blindingly bright and civilized. Dr. MacTavish looked up from where she was inserting locator disks and immediately took charge.

"Over there, on the table," she indicated, pushing her current patient away.

"He was—it was electrocution," Michael said, disbelieving even as he said the words.

The middle-aged doctor leaned over Gabe, lifting up an eyelid and looking; Michael hadn't even realized when his eyes had closed. Why wasn't she looking at the burn, on his leg? She grabbed a stethoscope and listened to his heart. Her face went taut. Then she began percussing Gabe's chest as hard as she could, hands clasped together. It looked like she was going to break his ribs.

She listened to the heart again.

She bit her lip and began percussing again.

Irene slipped into the room, unnoticed by the doctor, and nodded at Michael.

MacTavish listened to the stethoscope.

Then she put it down.

"He's dead," she said bluntly, but there was pain on her face.

"No," Michael said immediately. Calmly. "Impossible. Try again."

"He's. Dead. Want a listen?" she snapped, holding the stethoscope out to him. Then her face softened. "His heart must have stopped a few minutes ago. . . . He was already going cold when you brought him in."

Michael collapsed into a chair, unable to cry, unable to tear his eyes from Gabe.

Gabe.

Just a few minutes ago they had been talking.

Just a few hours ago they were taking a break from work with Liza, lying on the edge of the woods, tossing nuts down the hill and talking about life. It was warm and sleepy and philosophical and wonderful.

Just a day ago Michael had been in the middle of an adventure with him, which went from sunflowers to dead towns to alarmed warehouses to . . . finding *Finch* dead.

A circle of death, he realized. *Completed.*

It was insane to think that yesterday they had been at a mall, joking and laughing with Keely, eating crappy, amazing cereal out of old boxes. He still had the deodorant in his pocket. *Gabe* had given it to him.

It was ridiculous—no, it was *mad* that Gabe was gone, would never laugh or joke or kiss Keely again. It was a mistake.

"I should have been faster," Michael finally said, seeing

the corpse before him and feeling the crush of reality.

"I don't think it would have mattered," Dr. MacTavish said gently. "What—exactly—electrocuted him?"

"The electric fence. The one we were installing. The one I insisted on."

"O . . . kay . . ." Dr. MacTavish looked around, obviously inexperienced in this sort of grief. She spotted Irene with obvious relief. "Could you . . . ?" She jerked her head at Michael.

Irene nodded and went over. "Where were you, anyway?" Dr. MacTavish whispered.

"Research lab. Dr. Slattery," Irene whispered back. The other woman looked annoyed but didn't comment on it.

Irene came over and took Michael's hand. "It's not your fault."

"I didn't think I turned it on . . ." he mumbled. His thoughts raced. No, wait—he *had* turned it on. Just to make sure the feedback was working on the computer side. To make sure that he could read the proper voltages and *tell* when it was on or off. But he had turned it off, hadn't he? He thought he had. Michael moved his fingers as he thought back, trying to re-create what he'd done.

"Michael?" Liza came in the door as the two "paramedics," no longer needed, slipped out. Irene disappeared back into the corner, giving them some privacy. "Oh my GOD . . ." She saw Gabe and covered her mouth, trying not to scream.

"I did it," Michael said stonily. "It's my fault."

"Oh, Michael," Liza said softly, and knelt down, hugging him.

He couldn't stop the tears any longer and began to sob.

Later, after Irene and Nurse Chong had wrapped up the body and quietly removed it, Michael was left with two things: a hollowness in his soul and one last horrible task that he had to perform himself because it was his duty, his fault.

"Come on," he said wearily, taking Liza's hand. "I have to go tell Keely. She . . . liked Gabe." It sounded so stupid. So wooden. So *teenagey*. He thought back on how watching them kiss had kind of pissed him off and was horribly ashamed. The two walked hand in hand over to North Dorm, a strange reversal of the morning: now their heads were bowed, it was dark, and there was almost no one outside.

Each step inside up to the third floor, Michael thought his heart would stop working, just like Gabe's. It was even worse when he knocked and opened Keely's door—she was by herself, reading a book, and looked up at them with pleasure.

"Hey, guys!" Then she saw the looks on their faces. "What's . . . up?"

"Keely," Michael said slowly, taking a deep breath, "Gabriel is dead."

Liza knew she should have been thinking about Gabe, or Michael, or Keely, but all she could focus on was what a jealous idiot she had been. Keely was still crying, doing everything she could to stop it but failing. Michael held her, silent tears once again leaking out of his own eyes. *How could I have been such a jerk?* Liza had been *so jealous* of Keely getting to go on that trip.

But looking at the two of them in each other's arms, she *still* felt a pang of jealousy and was completely disgusted with herself. *I am a terrible person.*

"Keely, it's all my fault," Michael said.

"It was an accident," Keely said, generous to a fault. If it had been Liza, she would have been all over him about getting her boyfriend killed.

"I just don't understand," he said, frustrated. "I never even *activated* the Perry program."

"The what?" Keely asked.

"Perry program—it's what Frank called the electric fence software. 'Perimeter program.'"

Liza suddenly felt an icy grip on her stomach.

"I set it up and tested the controls but never let it go active. I've gone over what I did again and again, and I'm sure of it. It must have been some weird surge, some glitch—it was off again right after."

It couldn't have been.

Uncle Frank. Switching between the topo map and the other program—the Perry program. Right after Gabe and Michael left. The little dots moving on the topo program, closer and closer to the perimeter line. The numbers at the top of the screen.

It must have been a mistake. An accident.

"You guys want to take a walk?" she asked in a

strained voice. "I find . . . the clock tower is a good place to think about things."

"Liza, what the hell are you talking about?" Michael snapped. She realized it must have sounded like an incredibly flaky thing to say, like that old girlfriend he was always complaining about.

But Keely was looking at her strangely, like she saw something there. "Michael . . . I think that sounds like a good idea. . . . I could use some air."

"Let's go," Liza said as her hands started to tremble with the impossible thoughts filling her head.

FORTY-EIGHT

THERE WERE ONLY ABOUT FIVE MORE PEOPLE LEFT TO INSERT locator disks into that night, and Irene was almost too exhausted to handle them. *I'm not made for cloak-and-dagger,* she thought. And certainly not for lying. Her eyes flicked to the innocuous manila folders that waited patiently for her on the desk.

Sterilize. Slice. Insert. Sterilize. Bandage. *Too bad we don't have lollipops to give out.*

"Daddy," she said, recognizing the arm before looking up and recognizing the man.

"Hey, kiddo." Her dad broke all doctor-patient-relationship protocol by grabbing and hugging her. "You look so . . . *professional!*"

"It's the closest I'll ever get to being a doctor in this

day and age," Irene said, grinning. Aaron stuck his tongue out at her, but he was smiling too.

"And you're doing a *great* job." He held out his arm again. She tried not to behave any differently than she had with any other patient but found herself dabbing the alcohol on more gently.

"Daddy," she said, looking up briefly to make sure there was no one else in the room. "There's something weird going on with Diego. They've . . . stopped giving him antibiotics. And they've put him on happy pills."

"Maybe it's too late to do anything." But the concern on his face was for Irene, not the boy. Diego had been a prickly subject between them since they first found him in the woods, wounded, over a month ago. The fact that Irene had stayed behind to take care of him and later made her way *with him* to Novo Mundum made her dad uncomfortable whenever Diego came up in conversation.

"I . . . I stole his file, Daddy." She could hear Amber mentally yelling at her. *Trust no one!* "Something weird is going on."

"Irene, why would you do something like that?" Her father's face darkened with anger. "The three of us have found paradise here. Why would you want to jeopardize that? Especially after everything we've already lost."

Locator disks. Loony patients. No medical supplies and a traitor doctor. "I'm not sure this *is* paradise, exactly," Irene said before she could stop herself.

"This is the best place left on the planet. It's *crap* out there, or don't you remember?" Irene shrank back, letting go of Aaron's wrist. Her father had *never* talked to her that way, not even after her mom died and he freaked out for several weeks, destroying some of their furniture in the process. It was a scary time, but he never even once raised his voice at her and Aaron. This was just weird. *He's changed,* Irene realized. "I won't hear you disrespecting it *or* Dr. Slattery again!"

It was almost like some button had been pushed, a trigger activated—as soon as she'd tried to suggest something wasn't right, her dad became a stranger. As if he were . . . brainwashed.

Oh God. Were things even worse here than she'd thought?

"Yes, Daddy," she said calmly, trying to avert her gaze so he wouldn't realize how terrified she was. She took her brother's arm again and sliced it open. "I'm sorry, I'm really exhausted."

Her father's face lightened a little. "They must really depend on you, huh? Well, come back home as soon as you're done. I'll make us some matzoh brei. Okay?"

Irene nodded and only half pretended to stifle a yawn. Her dad kissed her on the forehead as he left and Aaron mouthed, *Come home soon.* She would. She had to figure out what the deal with her dad was. But first . . .

She got up quickly and locked the door as soon as they were gone, then moved the wastebasket so it blocked the door that led into the rest of the hospital. If someone tried to come through it, at least she'd have some warning. Finally she opened one of the files that had been taunting her for hours—Diego's first.

The handwriting was outrageous, almost impossible

to read. Probably Dr. Slattery's, if the joke about doctors held true. Earlier on, the notes were perfectly readable—MacTavish's, she assumed. *Basic penicillin and ten percent topical antibiotic cream on wound.* These were the earlier notes.

The later notes were harder to fathom: *Stop all treetmnts. Talky-wandrin round, give sedative. Healthy enough for Oct. and ennea strns. mve patnt to rsrch wng asap. 30ccs ennea.*

October . . . Oct . . . okt! That was Greek for eight. And *ennea* was Greek for nine. . . . Irene counted on her fingers to double-check. Yep. Nine. "Healthy enough for 8 and 9 strains."

Irene suddenly shuddered, remembering what Diego said. Patients with blackened skin. Like an advanced Strain 7. Like a Strain 8 or 9.

"Oh my God," she realized aloud. Dr. Slattery was developing new strains of the virus that had wiped out half the world! Diego was probably right about the sick people he'd seen . . .

And he was probably the next test subject.

FORTY-NINE

"WHAT IS THIS ALL ABOUT, LIZA?" MICHAEL DEMANDED WHEN they were finally at the top of the tower. It was spooky and cold; the breeze rifled through the workings of the clock and somehow wound up making the inside of the tower feel colder than it had outside. "Why are we here?"

"I had to take you guys someplace we could talk in private," Liza said.

"And a bench in the park wouldn't do?" he asked with so much sarcasm that even Keely stared at him. "What's so 'secret' you want to hide it from random Novo Mundians walking by?"

Liza took a deep breath. Now that she'd brought them here, she wasn't even entirely sure she wanted to share her fear. Saying it out loud would make it real, and that was the last thing in the world she wanted. But still, having to hold it in and handle it all herself wasn't proving to be any easier. She opened her mouth and forced the words out. "At the same time you and Gabriel were checking out the line," she began, "Uncle Frank was playing around with those programs you installed. I don't think he saw me, behind the bookshelves."

"I don't get it—what are you saying?" Michael asked, putting his hands on her shoulders.

"I saw that map program, the one that looks like a sort of a cartoony version of Novo Mundum from the top down. There were two little dots on it, blinking in and out and moving up the screen like radar, leaving little trails behind them. There were numbers at the top of the screen that also blinked. Then he switched to another program—the Perry one, I guess—and switched back and forth between the two programs before turning the whole thing off and leaving the room."

"Do you remember what the numbers were?" Michael asked slowly.

Liza shook her head. "All I know is that he was using those programs at the same time you guys were out there. It was an accident, I'm sure. I just don't want him getting in trouble," she said quickly.

"Liza . . ." Michael said gently. "Are you *sure* he was at the computer when it happened?"

She nodded, biting her lip. Tears were forming in her eyes.

"Let's go look at the computers," Keely suggested, strain sounding through her calm voice. "There will be a log, or user information, or *something* about who last used the programs or when—right?"

"It really was probably an accident," Liza said one more time. "I mean, it had to be."

FIFTY

Although he had spent all day working on installing the electric fence wires out in the woods, Jonah didn't complain about going back to his normal duties in the evening. Everyone had to pitch in; that was just the way it was. He had some ideas about the plumbing in the research building that might simplify things, based on what the ancient Romans used to do. If they could pump water without electricity, then so could Novo Mundum—all he needed was an afternoon of research. He bet the library had a bunch of books on engineering.

He ducked under a lab bench, frowning at one of the many mazes of tiny chrome piping. Was it really necessary to have water available at this bench? *If I can turn it off, that means more pressure for the ones down the line. . . .*

"Damn it, I'm *really* not happy about what happened to Gabriel. . . ." Dr. Slattery's voice came down the hallway along with the unmistakable thwacking sound of a rubber glove being taken off.

"He was getting too smart. And too flip. His attitudes toward Novo Mundum were well known."

That was Frank Slattery.

"You just keep doing what you're doing and let me run the show. Don't I always get you all the guinea pigs you need? And you're getting a new one today, by the way. Would have gotten two if there was anything left of Gabe."

Guinea pigs? "Would have gotten two if there was anything left of Gabe"?

Jonah felt cold horror trickle down his back when he realized what it meant. They were talking about *human* guinea pigs. What would they need them for?

"I'm making real progress, Frank," Dr. Slattery said excitedly.

"Whatever. Just make sure there are vaccines, too."

The two brothers continued arguing and walking down the hallway, past the room where Jonah was working. He didn't emerge until the double doors in front of the stairs slammed reassuringly closed.

What were they testing? Why were they using people? That didn't sound like something Dr. Slattery would do—Jonah knew him. It wasn't like the man at all. He was dedicated to *preserving* life. All of mankind.

That's why he was working on vaccines, like Frank Slattery had said. Maybe that was it. Maybe they were using corpses, not living people, to make new vaccines for Strain 7.

Jonah thought about his discussions with Dr. Slattery and the man's lectures to the community. One thing was for certain: whatever it was he was doing, it could only be for the good of Novo Mundum.

He went back to work, uncomfortable but determined.

FIFTY-ONE

WHEN THEY ASKED AROUND FOR "UNCLE FRANK," EVERYONE told Keely, Liza, and Michael that he was meeting with his brother over in the research lab. Michael told a version of the truth—that he was going in to see if he was responsible for the "accident." None of the guards gave him trouble. They gave Keely a sideways look but didn't say anything and just ignored Liza, who'd always had free run of the grounds.

While Michael booted up the computer, Keely looked at the manual for the electric fence software and Liza looked on, worried.

"According to the log, Frank was on and using those two programs at the time we were out there," Michael said, frowning at the screen.

"I *said* he was," Liza said, a little put out. Michael smiled and patted her knee.

"I'll just pull up the last map from the temp file. . . ."

The topographic map appeared, with two sets of dotted tracks approaching the crude line that Michael had drawn in the day before to represent the fence. At the end were two bigger dots, almost on top of the fence line. At the top of the page were two numbers, each corresponding to one of the dots.

420004 and 420005.

His and Gabe's locator disk codes. The map was last saved at 6:05.

Silently Michael pulled up the Perry program. The log showed that the electric fence had been activated for a span of eleven minutes at the full five thousand volts, starting at 6:01 and manually turned off at 6:12.

"He was trying to kill both of you, at the same time, by turning the fence on when you were near it." Keely said aloud what the other two didn't want to.

"No," Liza said stubbornly. "He would *never* do that. *Why* would he do that?"

Keely looked at Michael. "Because you told him there was a saboteur in Novo Mundum . . ."

"And he *is* the saboteur," Michael finished grimly. "He must have been the one Finch was trying to warn us about. It's perfect, really—Frank's in the perfect position to get messages to the outside world, and no one questions what he does. But why would he turn on his own brother?"

"This is all *crazy,*" Liza said again, trying not to cry.

"Uncle Frank would never sabotage Novo Mundum, or Dad, or murder someone, or anything."

"Did they ever fight?" Michael asked patiently. "Like, *really* fight about anything? Any deep philosophical disagreements or anything like that?"

"No. Uncle Frank always supported Daddy in everything. He told Daddy to get on with the real work while he took care of everything else, all the day-to-day stuff in Novo Mundum." Then Liza sort of smiled, sniffing. "Except for the electric fence. Uncle Frank was always pushing for that stupid electric fence. He and Daddy used to have yelling fights about it. My dad said it wasn't necessary. . . ."

"You don't think Frank called in those soldiers to *prove* Novo Mundum needed better defenses, do you?" Keely asked.

Michael nodded, thinking the same thing.

"And then tried to cover it up when we figured out it was an inside job."

"Why would he do it?" Liza said again, hopelessly, looking at the evidence against her uncle on the screen. There was no way to get around what he had done. "You could have been killed too," she suddenly realized, grabbing Michael's hand.

"What important work?" Keely suddenly said.

Michael and Liza looked at her.

"I mean, besides running Novo Mundum, which apparently Frank does most of, what important work? What exactly does your dad do in his labs?"

"He's—he's working on vaccines," Liza stammered.

"For what?" Keely pressed. "I thought everyone who survived 7 was basically genetically immune."

The two girls glared at each other for a moment, daring the other to back down.

"Vaccines for new strains," Liza finally admitted, looking down at the ground. "Strain 7 doesn't mutate easily, but if it did . . ."

"It could kill everyone left on the planet," Keely whispered.

Liza nodded. "*That's* his important work. It's a secret. I'm not supposed to tell anyone. He doesn't want anyone at Novo Mundum to know about his concerns. He doesn't want to cause a panic or make people worry. . . ."

"'Not a worry,'" Michael said ironically. Then he shook his head. "Okay, I'll worry about that later. Your uncle was just trying to protect your dad's really important research by finding an excuse to get better security. No offense, Liza—he might have had the best of intentions, but he went about it in a really psychotic way. And trying to murder me and Gabe to cover it up . . ."

"I was there too when you warned him about the saboteur," Keely said grimly. "I wonder what he planned to do about *me*."

Michael's eyes widened

"I hadn't even thought of that. . . ." *Idiot. Just because she's a girl doesn't mean Frank would be any less willing to cover up his trail.*

"Since both of us are obviously still on his hit list and in danger, we need to figure out what to do *now*." Her face had turned stony and determined; rather than collapse at Gabe's murder, she was prepared to do something about it.

"I'll get word to my father," Liza said, surprising both Michael and Keely. Her jaw was set as she tried to handle the most adult and important decision of her life. She grabbed a sheet of computer paper and began to scribble. "If he's working in the lab, I can get this note to him through one of the assistants. I'll tell him to meet me in the clock tower, where I'll tell him the truth about Uncle Frank. Maybe . . . *he* can figure out what to do."

"We should also probably find a way to stop people from getting their locator disks inserted for now," Michael decided, tapping his lips. "Frank knowing where everyone is can only be trouble. I'll go tell Irene." He got up to go.

"I'll come," Keely said, following him. "I'm actually scheduled to get mine tomorrow now—I saw earlier that they moved me up, even with my arm."

Michael held her gaze, a silent understanding passing between them. There was definitely a reason Keely's insertion had been moved up, and it wasn't a happy one.

He leaned over and kissed Liza. "You're being really brave—it's going to be hard for your father to accept."

"I know." Liza nodded, her face red and swollen with tears. "I can't really accept it myself."

As he and Keely left, Michael couldn't help but think once again how much better Liza was at handling this than Maggie ever would have been. His ex would have gone to pieces, unable to listen to reason or act on her own.

"You okay?" he asked Keely quietly when they were

outside. He had even fewer doubts about her, but it was obvious she and Gabe had been close. . . .

"No, but I'll manage." She gave him a weak smile. "Fixing this will go pretty far in helping."

The clinic doors were locked, but there was a light on inside. Michael knocked. A moment later Irene stuck her head out, looking for all the world like a prairie dog. When she saw who it was, she relaxed a little and opened the door wider for them to come in.

"Hey," she said, nervous and exhausted at the same time. She closed and locked the door behind them. "What's up?"

"You have to stop putting the locator disks in," Michael said.

Irene frowned, as if she were trying to process what he said and it still made no sense.

"Frank Slattery tried to have me and Gabe killed by turning the electric fence on when we were near it—he's the traitor we've been worried about. Until Dr. Slattery deals with him, we should keep the number of people he can keep an eye on to a minimum. *He's* the saboteur—and *extremely* dangerous."

"Until *Dr.* Slattery deals with him?" Irene said with shocking heavy sarcasm, so rare for her. She held up a medical file and shook it in his face. "Your beloved Dr. Slattery has been doing tests on *new strains* of Strain 7 and using human guinea pigs to test it out."

"You mean he's been developing vaccines for them," Michael corrected gently.

"I mean he's been *creating* them," Irene snapped,

pointing at the lines she had been studying earlier. Michael took the paper from her and stared at it. "He has been developing Strains 8 and 9, both of which spread *much* more easily—and whose symptoms look a whole lot like those of the black plague."

"I thought the black plague was bacteria," Keely said, obviously focusing on the things she could understand.

"Which could easily be cured with one dose of antibiotics. This is a *virus* and virtually unstoppable unless you have a natural immunity or were given a vaccine."

"What the hell is going on here?" Keely said, frustrated. "A pair of homicidal, lunatic brothers running what is supposed to be the last, best hope for mankind's intellectual and spiritual development?"

"He must be developing it as a weapon in case the government ever attacks," Michael said, sitting down. He couldn't believe it. He just *couldn't*.

"Or creating a plague to wipe out the *rest* of humanity," Keely said bitterly.

"They're both control freaks," Irene said quietly. "They have this 'vision' of how the world and Novo Mundum should be, and they'll do anything to protect it."

"Maybe Frank knew what was going on and called in the soldiers to *stop* his brother," Michael said slowly.

"Or maybe *Finch* knew what was going on and volunteered to go with MacCauley's soldiers to warn the government," Keely suggested. "Frank suspected that and managed to kill them all in the jeep before they got away."

Michael shook his head. "No, it was with a rocket

launcher, remember? There are no high-power weapons at Novo Mundum."

"Yes, there are," Irene interrupted. "When I finally got in to see Diego, when I stole these, he told me about a cache of weapons like flamethrowers and stuff. He also said he *saw* Dr. Slattery's victims, all sick and dying."

"We have to get out of here." Keely shook her head at the insanity. "This place is crazy dangerous."

"Not before I get Diego," Irene said. "They're planning his first exposure to the virus tomorrow— I was just going to go get him when you guys showed up. I could use some help," she added, looking expectantly at them. "I don't think I can carry him alone if he's still drugged up."

"Keely, you take this and go warn Liza." Michael handed her the folder. "She'll never believe you otherwise. I'll go with Irene to get Diego—we'll meet back together in three hours. . . ."

"In the kids' art classroom," Keely suggested. "It will be unlocked, and no one's going to be there at this time of night."

"All right," Michael said grimly. "Let's go."

FIFTY-TWO

Diego dreamed he was in a hospital where people were dying and the doctors were murdering them. He tried to scream, but nothing would come out. It didn't matter; he was strapped to a bed and he couldn't escape.

Then he woke up.

He was in a hospital where the murmurs of sick people with decaying bodies could not be shut out because his hands were tied to the sides of his bed and he couldn't cover his ears. He opened his mouth to scream, to cover the noise of the people he could not help with some noise of his own. Nothing came out.

Then he woke up.

❊   ❊   ❊

A boy who looked familiar lay in a hospital gurney, trying to remember what to fear. He was alone, but for some reason that was okay. The dead and dying were not far from him, yet that wasn't what he was supposed to be afraid of.

Nurse Chong leaned over and smiled at him.

"Looks like the new tests have been moved up, lucky boy! We'll get you out of here."

As she wheeled him through the door, Diego tried to scream.

But nothing came out.

FIFTY-THREE

THERE WASN'T EVEN ANYONE IN THE HOSPITAL SIDE OF THE quarantine section; Irene and Michael were able to get there unseen, with only a pause to put on gloves and a mask.

"Which room is he in?" Michael asked, poking his head into one of the rooms through the plastic flaps.

"It's not any of these; it's an office, closer to the research lab side."

"You're sure these will protect us?" he asked a little nervously, squinting at the mask.

"I doubt the virus is even floating around; if he's been this good at concealing it from the rest of Novo Mundum, it's probably very well contained. And yes, these will protect us." She didn't mention the possibility of an anthrax-type virus that could infect you through your skin; she tried not to think about it herself.

As they approached the doors to the research labs, Irene was already planning how she and Michael would carry Diego out. Then she stopped short.

"Oh no," she whispered, unable to believe it.

There were guards on the other side of the door. What terrible, terrible luck—what were the chances that Dr. Slattery would be working on something right when they needed to get in?

The two men were completely disguised from head to toe in decontamination suits, so like what the armies of decon units wore when they came to steal and burn the dead. Inside those suits were probably two very normal, nice Novo Mundians, but Irene had no idea who they were or how to talk to them.

"Wait. . . ." She went over what she had just thought. "I think I have an idea. . . ."

After Michael helped her into the bulky haz-mat suit, he gave her a thumbs-up and headed down to the entrance on the first floor, where he would wait for her to unlock the door from the other side.

Irene took a deep breath. In movies, whenever anyone attempted anything like this, you always knew that they were going to succeed and never really cared about what the character was thinking. *She* had no idea if it was going to work, and if she failed, not only would Diego be lost, but she would probably become a human guinea pig herself.

Death. Death if she failed.

She took a deep breath. *I'm not the brave one. Why the hell is it me?* And opened the door.

The two guards turned, guns up. She couldn't even see their eyes. But of course, they couldn't see hers either. Irene coughed explosively and then said in a croaking voice,

"Is my dad in there?"

Wait. Did Liza say dad or daddy? Probably daddy. Oh, hell . . .

The two guards relaxed. One of them nodded, which looked a little ridiculous in the big hood he wore. "He's upstairs," he said. "But I think he's busy. You'll have to wait in his office."

"Thanks," Irene said in a hoarse voice, coughing again. She was shaking inside the suit, another likely symptom of whatever she supposedly had.

They bought it. In fact, as she toddled off toward the stairs at the end of that hall, she could hear them muttering about how awful it was that she had been in quarantine twice that week.

"Probably got a cold playing tonsil hockey with that new guy," one of them said. "He was out on some sort of mission for a few days."

The other laughed, but not unkindly.

Ewww. But Irene made herself think about tonsil hockey with Michael because it kept her from fainting or thinking about what she was doing. He was a nice enough guy and smart and all but so type A. . . . He probably would have been a management consultant or something equally high powered and evil if Strain 7 hadn't happened.

As soon as she turned the corner and the guards were out of sight, she started looking for Diego, reasoning that he had to be on the same floor because of the gurney. There were no working elevators, not even in the research lab.

The first couple of rooms were the ones where she'd found the notebooks and files—otherwise they were empty. Farther on there were handwritten signs posted here and there that warned about viral safety procedures.

Getting closer.

She finally found him.

He was lying on his back, his arms and legs tied down. A surgical mask covering his mouth made for a makeshift gag. He was awake and tried to scream when he saw her, the whites of his eyes showing.

"Diego, it's me," she whispered, taking off the hood so he could see.

His eyes closed in relief, and tears began to form.

"Michael and I are going to get you out of here. I *promise*. I'll be back in five minutes, okay? You wait here."

Irene expected him to protest, but he nodded, understanding. Looking brave. It was the hardest thing in the world to leave him, but there was no way she was getting him out without Michael's help. She leaned over and kissed him quickly on the cheek for reassurance before leaving.

Downstairs was uninhabited—everyone at dinner or home. Not even the clinking of labware. She lumbered to the locked door that led back to the hospital wing and opened it. Michael was waiting, having ripped apart the boards that had been used to seal up the entrance.

"I found him," she said.

"Might as well take that thing off," Michael said, indicating the suit. "If we get caught now, the trick ain't gonna work twice, and we need to move fast."

Reluctantly Irene stripped the haz-mat suit off, shedding the only layer of protection and concealment from the evils that lay in the research wing.

They ran lightly down the corridor together—then froze. A soft thumping sound came from one of the labs, like someone reshelving books. They ducked into the closest room and waited, barely breathing.

Irene cursed herself—it had already been longer than the five minutes she had promised Diego.

After what seemed like *hours,* a person finally emerged from the lab, whistling and tossing some keys up into the air and catching them in his lab coat pocket. Young, happy—*and helping to develop a virus to destroy the rest of the world.*

They had just stepped out into the corridor when another person came out of the lab, headed right for them.

Both sides stopped.

"Dr. MacTavish?" Irene said, wondering how she was going to talk her way out of this one. But the other woman looked equally surprised and guilty. She carried another box of supplies.

"Get in here!" she hissed, indicating the lab again. Irene and Michael followed, unquestioning, unsure what else to do. "What the hell are you doing here?" the doctor demanded in a harsh whisper.

"What are *you* doing here?" Michael countered.

"You tell me first, or I'll turn you in. You have *far* less of a right to be here than I do," the doctor threatened.

"You've been stealing things from Dr. Slattery's lab," Michael countered. "Irene's *seen* you. You tell us what you're up to or we'll tell him."

There was a long moment of silence. Irene tried not to breathe as the two stood there, each not backing down.

"I'm stealing supplies, you ninny," the doctor finally said, rolling her eyes. "Slattery's research lab has commandeered all sorts of stuff—like antibiotics for your friend Diego." She looked knowingly at Irene. "And bandages and antiseptic solution . . . and almost every palliative you can name. Everything the hospital could use. What the labs need it for is—well, you can only guess. The only reason your precious Diego ever got any real antibiotics at all was because I stole some. *Okay?* And what about *you?*"

Irene and Michael exchanged embarrassed looks. So Dr. MacTavish, their number-one suspect, had turned out to be one of the good guys. *Possibly the* only *good guy,* Irene realized.

"We're trying to rescue Diego," Michael said grudgingly. "It seems that Dr. Slattery has been trying to *create* new viruses and needs human test subjects."

"Wait. What?" the doctor asked.

"I went through the lab and Diego's files." Irene finally spoke up, calmly. "The October Project he's been working on is essentially a Strain 8. He's also developing a 9."

"Holy crap," Dr. MacTavish said, blinking. "And because Diego was damaged and not even chosen to join, of course he would serve as a guinea pig. It could have been *you*." She pointed at Michael. He looked surprised. "I don't think you fully understand their attitude toward non–Novo Mundians," she added dryly.

"They had him on phenobarbital," Irene said quietly. "I found a vial on the floor."

"They probably started giving it to him as soon as they took him from the public quarantine area," the doctor said slowly, nodding. "The last time I was allowed to see him, Diego *was* kind of out of it and hard to wake up." Then she shook her head. "*New* strains of the virus? That's beyond evil. That's madness. What does Slattery hope to accomplish?"

Irene shrugged helplessly.

"A last-resort weapon against the government, maybe," Michael said.

"Can I see the files?" Dr. MacTavish asked. "Maybe you're wrong; maybe you don't understand what he's saying. . . ."

"We gave it to Keely," Irene said, "but it was pretty straightforward."

There was another long moment's silence between the three, but no tension this time.

"You guys are going to have to leave here, you understand," Dr. MacTavish finally said. "Once you get Diego. You can't do *anything* around here without someone finding out about it—everyone's watching everyone else."

"Come with us," Irene said impulsively. "You're obviously not happy here anyway. . . ."

The doctor looked at her a long moment, hope kindling in her eyes. Then her face darkened. "Thanks," she said gently. "But I think I'm more needed here. At the very least, I can find out what's really going on. At the most, I can try to do something about it."

"If they catch you, you'll wind up like Gabe or Finch or Diego," Michael pointed out.

Dr. MacTavish shrugged and flashed them a sad smile. "Hippocratic oath, sonny boy. I'll save as many lives as I can. And not administer any 'deadly drugs.' Never understood that part of it . . . Well, good luck, chickadees, whatever you decide to do. Irene, you'll make a great doctor someday. It might not have shown, but I really liked working with you. Oh, and if you're going back through the second-floor doors, you should know that there was a maintenance worker down there—I think he was finishing up, but just in case, keep your ears peeled."

The doctor saluted them, then toddled off with her box.

Irene had the sinking feeling it would be the last time she would see the grouchy dermatologist. *I should have gotten to know her better instead of just suspecting her every move.* She marked it in her mind as an important lesson.

Michael just shook his head. "I guess you never know."

When it was safe, they went back out to the hall and continued to the stairs and up to the second-floor hall, once again hiding—this time as the hooded haz-mat-suit wearers changed guard. As soon as they got to

Diego, Irene took his gag off and Michael undid his restraints.

"Not a dream . . ." Diego murmured.

"Yeah, but we're also not out yet, so cut the chatter until we are," Michael said, giving him a grin. Diego smiled weakly back.

"Up!" Irene ordered, and with their help Diego managed to sit up and swing his legs over the side of the gurney.

"And *down.*" Michael and Irene each put one of his arms around their shoulders and hoisted him off the table, keeping his feet off the floor.

The weight was incredible—Irene was small, like Liza, and not particularly strong. But now wasn't the time to give in. She gritted her teeth and stood straight—thank God Michael had come along.

"Easy now," Michael whispered. "Try to lean most of your weight on me."

The three of them clumsily made their way through the door sideways and down the hall—like two angels, one good and one bad, helping Diego along. They paused at the stairs, giving Irene a breather as he balanced on his good left leg and Michael started down.

"Sorry about this, Diego, but it's the easiest way," Michael said, putting his shoulder to the other boy's waist and throwing him over his shoulder. "Second time I've had to do this today," Michael grunted. He gripped the rail for support and carefully felt his way down the stairs, to the landing, and down the other stairs. Irene practically leapt behind; without Diego's weight on her shoulder she felt like she was floating.

"Just a little bit farther," Michael promised, setting him gently down at the bottom. Irene got under his other shoulder again.

Just twenty more feet. Irene looked down the shiny black linoleum hall and counted down the steps. *Eighteen feet and then we're safe.* Of course, that was far from the truth. She had no idea what they would do *after* they got out of the research lab. Leave, like Dr. MacTavish had said? In the middle of the night, with no supplies? Where would they *go?*

Michael stumbled and Diego's foot hit the floor with a sickeningly loud thump as he attempted to balance himself.

There was a noise from one of the rooms, the sound of someone pushing back a chair and standing up—maybe to investigate. Irene and Michael quickly dragged Diego into another room. A door opened down the hallway and footsteps came directly toward where they were hiding.

Without stopping to think about it, Irene went out to meet whoever it was; maybe she could buy the others some time to go—at least she had a *slightly* better right to be there than Michael and Diego.

"Irene . . . ?"

She turned to meet the person full-on, prepared for the worst.

It was Jonah.

FIFTY-FOUR

When Keely finally found Liza, she was out of breath from having run all over campus. The other girl was already walking toward the clock tower to wait for her dad.

"Liza, stop," Keely wheezed. "You can't meet with your father."

"What are you talking about?"

Keely held up the manila folder. She knew what she was about to say would destroy Liza, and normally she wouldn't be so blunt—but lives were at stake here, including her own, and there was just no time to find a right way to say this. Besides, it wasn't like there could really be one, anyway. "Your dad is not just creating vaccines," she blurted. "He's also creating viruses themselves, to use as a weapon or something." She didn't add her private theory: that when cult leaders feel they are beginning to lose control of an organization, they tend to enforce mass suicide or death.

"I don't believe you," Liza said coldly. Just like out of a TV show. *Then again, her beliefs have already been pushed to the limit today,* Keely realized.

"Take this," Keely said, shoving the folder into her hands. "*Look* at it. Whether or not you believe it right now, understand that Dr. Slattery"—she very carefully didn't say *your dad*—"and his brother are not to be trusted. They each have their own agenda. And both of them seem to involve violence."

Liza continued to glare at her, but there was uncertainty and fear in her eyes.

"Liza," Keely tried again. "I know you don't like me." The other girl started to automatically protest, but Keely rolled her eyes and cut her off. "It's true. And believe me, if I could have had Michael or *anyone* else tell you this, I would have. Just *look* at it."

The other girl slowly, tentatively took the folder. Keely realized with instant regret that Liza was going to *take it with her* to read. Probably a bad move on her own part to hand it over—the girl might show it to her dad, throw it out, make off with it. It was their only evidence of what was really going on at Novo Mundum.

"You're asking me to believe that my dad is making viruses and killing people with them," Liza said bleakly.

"I'm not asking you to believe anything right now. I'm asking you to be careful when talking to your dad—for your own sake," Keely said. "This may mean your uncle is innocent," she added. "Maybe he told the government something was going on in order to stop your dad."

A faint ray of hope appeared in Liza's eyes. "Where *is* Michael?" she finally asked.

"He and Irene are rescuing our friend Diego, who's next in line to be used as a human guinea pig for Strain 8 or 9 or something."

Liza looked at Keely's face, obviously searching for some clue that there was an escape from this truth but not finding one.

"All right," Liza agreed reluctantly.

FIFTY-FIVE

"Jonah," Irene said, too surprised to say much else. "Thank *God.*"

"What are you doing here?" Jonah asked, obviously torn between being glad to see her and worried that she was in an off-limits area.

"I need to talk to you, actually—can we go in there?" She indicated the room Jonah had come from and started walking toward it without waiting for him.

He followed and closed the door behind him.

"What's this all about?"

"Jonah, I—" She took a deep breath. "I know how you feel about Dr. Slattery and Novo Mundum, but there are some pretty terrible things going on here you should know about."

"Like what?" But he said it guardedly. Almost like he *knew* . . .

"Like that Dr. Slattery is *engineering* new viruses as a weapon or something," she said gently. "And he's testing them out on people."

"No, he's making vaccines. He's testing *those* out on people," he corrected her.

He knew? He knew about the testing? Irene wondered in surprise and horror. *And he doesn't seem to be that upset. . . .*

"It's sad, but it's got to be done, to keep us safe," he said, equally gently.

"No, Jonah, he *really is* making these viruses. We have proof—and he was going to test one out on *Diego.*"

Jonah looked a little taken aback at *that,* at least.

"That's terrible," he said quietly. "But the needs of the many outweigh the needs of the few or the one."

"Don't quote *Star Trek* at me!" Irene snapped. "These are *real* people's lives! Real friends of yours!"

"Who are guaranteeing the quality of life for the rest of us. It's horrible, but I'd do it too. If I was too sick to be treated, I'd volunteer myself so that other people could live."

Irene stepped back, disbelieving.

"What are you doing here?" he repeated, refusing to discuss the subject further. She had to change tracks quickly.

"Stealing some bandages for the hospital," she said with a wry, embarrassed grin. She felt *terrible* lying to him, but—he was lost, this much was obvious. "We requisitioned some earlier but need them now—some people are getting infections from the disk procedure."

Jonah studied her face. Could he tell that she was lying? The fact that she didn't actually *have* any bandages might be a clue. . . .

"You should get out of here," he said sadly. "You shouldn't come back in here again."

"I—I know."

He leaned over and kissed her on the cheek.

"Novo Mundum is the best thing that ever happened to me," he whispered, "and it might be the best thing that ever happened to the world. Whatever's going on, I'm happy here."

"I know," Irene repeated, staring up into his face. If things were different, maybe she could have liked Jonah—the way he wanted her to. Handsome, smart, caring, and earnest . . . This was just the wrong time and the wrong place. The wrong side.

She turned and left, closing the door behind her.

Michael and Diego had already made it out and through the doors back into the hospital, but it didn't matter; Jonah waited a good long time before opening the door and making sure she was gone.

FIFTY-SIX

LIZA LOOKED THROUGH THE PAPERS AS SHE WAITED FOR HER dad in the drafty, cold clock tower, wishing she had brought a sweater this time. She couldn't make out a lot of the terminology, but she could read her dad's handwriting better than the others could. And there were definitely paragraphs devoted to the rate of growth of viruses and which strains died when exposed to certain temperatures, bleach, Lysol, and other things. And which strains couldn't be killed by easy methods.

Was her father really doing this? Was he planning to use them as a weapon if the government attacked? *Was it really worth the people he was testing it on?* Her dad always talked about sacrifice for progress, but she had never thought about it in terms of people she knew. Did

Uncle Frank really know what he was up to? Was he trying to save everyone?

She always called him Daddy. His pet name for her was Liza girl. He might not have been as close to her in some ways as Uncle Frank, but he was still *her dad.* Some of her earliest memories were of sitting in his lab, playing with models of bacteriophages and prions while he worked. When it was time for a break, he always let her get a bag of junk food out of the machine in the hall—something her mom *never* would have done. It was their little secret.

Footsteps on the stairs. Liza quickly crammed the folder into the woodwork behind the clock.

"Liza? Are you there? Liza? What's this all about?"

Her father came around the corner. He hadn't changed from this morning—still the same charismatic face, the piercing blue eyes, the easy smile. Did it look like *she* had changed? Could he see her suspicions?

Confronted with her dad, she found herself speechless.

I am not choosing between Dad and Michael.

I am not choosing between Dad and Uncle Frank.

"Liza girl! What's going on?" He put his arm out to draw her in.

"I think Uncle Frank's gone crazy!" she sobbed, hugging him back. It had been the first thing to find its way out of her mouth. Now the only question was what would come next.

Michael met Keely in the darkened art classroom.

"Where are Irene and Diego?" she asked, worried.

"They're safe, in an old equipment shack by the

tennis courts." Michael looked exhausted and sank down into one of the tiny kids' chairs.

"I think Frank's back at the computer," Keely said, also sitting. "I saw him marching toward Alumni Hall with Ellen."

"Great. He knows where *everyone* is now."

"Maybe he just went in to erase what he did to you and Gabe."

"Maybe, but we have to keep in mind that he can now see where at least a quarter of the people are at all times. *Including* me." He held up his arm.

They were both silent for a moment.

"What do we do now?" Keely asked, for both of them.

"This is all the food I could get you," Irene apologized as she picked her way around old tennis rackets and court-painting machines in the equipment shed where Diego was hiding. He sat on an old lawn chair in the corner, leg up, resting. Even in the darkness he looked a little healthier, free of the happy pills and whatever else he'd been given. *The body just needs time to heal itself.*

She sat down on the chair next to him and offered a few slices of rock-hard protein bread with an old Coke bottle filled with water.

"We'll get out of here, I promise," Diego said, holding her hand and squeezing it.

"Wow, the invalid makes plans," Irene said, laughing despite the sensation of her heart racing in her chest from adrenaline, panic, fear of what came next.

"I *promise*," he repeated.

Irene was suddenly aware of how *alone* they were in the tiny shed in the dark. Except for when she was sneaking around, she was never alone at Novo Mundum, even in the evening.

Diego was looking at her seriously, his aquiline profile outlined perfectly against the window.

He put a hand under her chin, turned her head, and brought it closer to his. Her breath caught as she gazed back into his eyes, their faces inches apart. Her heart still pounded like crazy, but not from fear. "Diego—" she began, but before she could finish, his lips were on hers. She moaned softly, and he deepened the kiss. He pulled her, gently, out of her chair and on top of him, wrapping his arms tightly around her. His hands moved up her back, her neck, seemingly everywhere at once and leaving behind an amazing warmth wherever they touched.

Irene felt herself melt into him. As she responded, his kiss grew stronger, more passionate. Suddenly *she* was safe, cared for, loved by someone else—someone she had fallen for the first moment she saw him, lying in the woods.

"I promise," he whispered one more time, breaking the kiss just long enough to say the words.

"What do you mean, he's *crazy?*"

What did she mean . . . ? If only Liza knew. But she had to say something, had to form words, sentences somehow. "I think he's responsible for the soldiers knowing where we are and Finch and all of that," she said quickly. "'Cause how would they know where to go, and he was always looking for some reason to force the whole electric fence issue, and . . ."

"And you think he would risk all of us for his crazy electric fence?" her father asked, smiling and touching her nose with the tip of his finger.

"Yeah, I do," Liza said. "He's been acting . . . weird recently. And the whole thing with Gabe being electrocuted . . ."

Her father looked grave, listening to her charges against his brother. But there was sorrow in his eyes.

Liza knew him too well. He was looking at her with pity. *Oh, dear, Liza's become a problem. . . .* But he wouldn't do anything to his own *daughter,* right?

As he hugged her, Liza only knew one thing: she didn't want to stick around long enough to find out. She had to leave Novo Mundum.

Now.